# Seventy Times Seven

### Fayla Ott

In loving memory of Arledge and Dorothy Murff

*Then Peter came to Jesus and asked, 'Lord, how many times shall I forgive my brother or sister who sins against me? Up to seven times?' Jesus answered, 'I tell you, not seven times, but seventy-seven times'.*
*Matthew 18:21-22*

*1*

Cotton is strongest when it's wet. I don't know how many times I heard Onnie say that. That phrase was as familiar to me as the deep, long scar across her sunken, brown cheek.

The first time I saw that scar was the summer of '79. I had just finished second grade. In those early days of my life, I often wondered away from my little shotgun house, with its peeling, white paint, and dark shutters. The porch had also seen better days. There was no lattice to surround the bottom, leaving the underneath exposed to reveal bricks, tools, and a broken ladder. That little house, like so many in the Mississippi Delta where I grew up, was surrounded by rows of cotton. The Delta landscape wasn't much more than cotton and soybean fields. Other than the Yazoo River, with its banks of muscadine grape vines and the occasional gator peeking up from its murky waters, there were small communities of post offices, gas stations and grocery markets, and what was known as Honky Tonks where the men—married or single—would gather on Saturday nights to engage in activities I wasn't supposed to understand.

That afternoon I decided to do something I'd never done. I crossed the railroad tracks at the wrong part of town. My cousins and I had often played on the tracks where they ran close to my grandfather's property, but we had never gone this far down, and we wouldn't have dreamed of going across the tracks and into what was known then as Color Town. Color Town wasn't really a town. It consisted of several rows of little houses with tiny porches, clotheslines draping off the end of them, with the occupants often sitting on old couches or broken chairs that no longer served a purpose inside the house. When I looked up and realized I was on the road that ran right in front of the first row of houses, fear seized my legs and I stopped. My gaze collided with a black man on a porch. He stared and I stared back. Color Town was off limits. My mama would have given me a whooping had she known where I stood.

The man had on one of those undershirts without sleeves. His arms were skinny and long. He held a fly swatter in one hand. On the floor of the porch sat a little boy. He had wide, dark eyes, and chubby cheeks. He wore only a diaper and sucked on the pacifier in his mouth. He stared at me, too, as if he'd never seen a white girl before. Maybe he hadn't.

I decided to keep walking in front of the houses. There was a field past the first row, and I could cut across that, then walk down the railroad tracks to the back of our property. My heart beat so fast that I couldn't hear my footsteps on the pavement over its thud in my chest.

"What are you doing here?" A tall group of boys stood on the side of the road. A couple of them had bandannas on their heads. The others had them tied around their blue jeans on their thighs. The one who spoke had one of those Afro hair styles and he had a laugh in his voice.

I didn't answer him. I wasn't supposed to talk to them. I stared at the field ahead but didn't run. I felt them before I saw them. The boys were suddenly there behind me, laughing and grabbing at my long, blond hair.

"That's some soft hair you have, girl." It was the Afro boy again. He had a handful of my hair. My heart beat faster, but this time it didn't compete with my footsteps. I couldn't move.

"Tyrone James, get away from that little white girl and go home before I call your grandma. She'll tan your hide." I turned and saw a tall, slender woman standing in the doorway of a house, holding the screen door open.

"Oh, c'mon, Miz Onnie, I ain't hurtin' nobody. We's just havin a lil' fun, that's all. She's the one who came up in Color town where she don't belong."

"You best get home where you belong. Right now. All of you."

The boys murmured as they sauntered off in the opposite direction where I was headed.

"Why you here, Suga?"

I looked back at the woman who had shooed off the boys. She had stepped to the edge of the porch, so I got a good look at her face. A deep scar stretched across her cheek from the side of her nose to her jawline. I couldn't speak. I only stared at this woman whose voice sounded nothing like I would imagine.

"You want some cookies, child? I don't have any fancy ones, just those store-bought vanilla kind with the cream inside, but you welcome to 'em. I have milk, too."

She held a dish towel in her hands. Her yellow dress had little blue flowers all over it, with a ruffle at the bottom. I just stood there, staring at her. I had never been inside a black person's home before. I'd get whipped for sure. But her voice sounded kind. Although her face scared me, her eyes didn't.

I finally answered her. "I have to go home now."

"Suit yourself. You're probably better off that way."

I nodded, then started walking. I looked back. She still watched me.

"You can change your mind, you know. Ain't no law against you eatin' my cookies. No real law, that is."

I liked how she talked to me. I surprised myself by walking back toward her house. For the first time, I noticed a difference between her house and the others on the street. Her house had flowerpots all over the porch. There was no old furniture, just a rocker and a table with more planters filled with various flowers.

She didn't say anything but turned and opened her screen door. I followed her inside. As soon as I walked in, I half expected my mama to come in after me, dragging me out by my soft hair.

I don't know what I expected to find inside. It looked much like my house. There was a television set with a pair of rabbit ears on top. There was a couch, a braided rug, and a table with a lamp. Nothing out of the ordinary.

I followed her into the kitchen. She opened a cabinet and pulled out a pack of sandwich cookies, then opened the refrigerator and lifted a carton of milk from the side door. I sat down at the small table that had been pushed against the wall to make more space.

"You gonna tell me what happened to your eye?" She asked, pouring the milk.

I looked down at the cookies and picked one up. Dipping it in the milk, I looked at her as I took a bite.

She watched me but didn't say anything.

"I fell down."

"Seems to me a mighty rough fall. You sure you didn't get any help?"

I knew what she meant but didn't answer. I looked out the window at two kids riding bikes. One stopped to fix his chain, slowly turning the pedals until the chain went back on its track.

"I've seen you before. You live over on that cotton farm, don't you? The one with all the fruit trees."

"No, ma'am. That's my grandparents' house. I live down the road from them."

"I've seen you playing with some boys in the front yard."

"Those are my cousins."

She nodded as if she already knew. "Is that who gave you that nasty bruise?"

I shrugged my shoulders and twisted one of the cookies. I scraped the cream out of one with my teeth, then dipped the rest into the milk before shoving it into my mouth.

"I'd better go home." I told her when I finished. "Thank you for the cookies."

"Aren't you going to tell me your name? I did slave over these cookies, you know." She winked and I smiled.

"Tara."

"Ah. Like that movie."

"Yes, my mama loves Gone with the Wind. She-" I stopped. I had heard black folks didn't like that movie.

She laughed. "It's alright, girl. I don't mind. It's just a movie. You can't expect movies to tell the truth, although I expect that one tells more truth than most people would like to admit, white or black." She laughed and shook her head. "You can call me Onnie."

"Is that your real name?"

"You'd think it was a nickname, wouldn't you? I wish I could say it came from Veronica or something fancy like yours, but it's just Onnie."

I didn't say so, but I liked it. It suited her.

"You don't have to be afraid to be here. Most folks around here just tryin' to make their way. They won't hurt you. Just stay away from Shiloh and you'll be fine."

Shiloh was another black neighborhood even further up the tracks. It was named after the creek that ran behind it. Those shack houses were even worse than the ones in Color Town.

As I was leaving, she handed me a napkin with another cookie in it. "For the road," she said. "Bring your cousins by for a visit."

I didn't tell her that I wouldn't tell a soul I'd been in Color Town.

But I knew I'd be back.

—————

My house wasn't big, but it wasn't much different than most houses in that area. In fact, my grandparents' house was the same down the road. Shotgun houses were common in the Delta. Papaw Webb said they were easier to build. When I asked him why it was called a shotgun house, he decided to show me. He took down his shotgun from the rack on the wall, had me prop open the screen door on the back of the house, and meet him at the front. Then, Papaw actually fired that shotgun from the front door, aiming at the back. I thought Mamaw Webb was going to snatch that gun right out of his hand and fire it right back at him. Instead, she took her straw broom and started swinging at him. He laughed at her as he grabbed it out of her hand. Papaw didn't talk a whole lot, but when he did, it was usually in a dramatic way that I'd remember. Once he threw a spoon at my cousin Albert when he mouthed off at the breakfast table. Albert enjoyed riling Papaw up and making us giggle behind our hands. Papaw was either laid back or hot headed. There was no in between. I didn't mind. It was easy to read his moods, so I knew how to behave.

"That bullet went straight through, Tara Gail. And that's why it's a shotgun house." With that, he put the gun back on the rack and went to his chair to watch the ball game on the television.

My own house looked sad when I approached. There were no flowers on the front porch. I heard Mama's voice in the kitchen. It had that lilted tone, which could only mean one thing. We had company.

A man sat at the table with my mama. He looked like that funny doctor on M.A.S.H. My mama never missed an episode. He had on a suit with one of those wide, plaid ties.

Mama saw me and said, "Where have you been? We have company. Just look at your muddy shoes."

"Hello, Tara. Your mama has told me all about you. I'm Reverend Martin, your new preacher. I'll be seeing you at church on Sunday."

I looked at Mama. She was looking at this stranger like he really was her hero from her favorite television show. Church? The only times we had ever gone was when Mamaw made Mama feel guilty for not raising me right. Whenever Mama tired of Mamaw's guilt trips, she'd bring me. Papaw never went, except for Easter Sunday. Everyone went to church on Easter Sunday.

The man thanked Mama for the coffee, rubbed the top of my head, and walked out the door. Mama picked up the coffee cups and placed them in the sink. As soon as his engine faded away, her face changed.

Her fist came down hard on my right cheek.

"How dare you embarrass me in front of the preacher, coming in here looking all filthy!" She placed one hand on my mouth, grabbed the back of my neck with the other and started pushing me through rooms. When we reached the bathroom, she shoved me into the tub. I fell backwards and hit my head against the tile wall. She pulled the shower curtain closed and turned the faucet on. Cold water sprayed over my body.

"You stay in there until that mud is gone. Don't you dare get out."

I did get out, but only when I figured she had forgotten about me. Shivering and soaked to the skin, I tiptoed to my room, wrapped in a towel. I undressed and changed into pajamas. That night, I didn't think I would ever get warm again.

The next day, I opened my eyes to see Mama smiling at me over my bed.

"Want some pancakes?"

# 2

My cousins were like chewing gum. Playing with them lost its flavor after a while, but I kept playing anyway. Albert, a husky boy for his age, liked to bully his younger brother and me. Sam was two years younger than Albert who was eleven. Sam wasn't exactly naughty like Albert, but he wasn't good, either. He didn't mind doing the wrong things, he just didn't like getting caught. Uncle Brody was their dad, and he didn't waste no time punishing his boys when they stepped out of line. Albert had made many trips to the peach trees to pick out his own switch. Every time my uncle whipped my cousins he'd say, "That's why the Good Lord gave you a behind." Uncle Brody played football with Albert, and he took both fishing and hunting. He'd get down in the floor and wrestle with all three of us on Mamaw's braided rug, too, until Papaw shouted, "Get out from in front of my TV!" Then Papaw would rise out of his chair and make a production out of straightening the "rabbit ears" antenna because their bouncing around had disturbed the clear picture. Uncle Brody would wink at the boys and me and then we'd go at it again until Papaw threw his slippers at us. Then, he'd head for the rabbit ears again.

Uncle Brody and my cousins lived with my grandparents on the cotton farm. My uncle worked for Holder's. It was a factory that built engines for trucks. Mama said he had a good paying job since he supervised a whole bunch of people over there, and she didn't know why Aunt Diane just "up and ran off" the way she did. Mamaw said a good paying job didn't matter much when he drank the money away. I wasn't supposed to know about my uncle's drinking problem, or how he ran his wife off by spending all their money on it. I wasn't supposed to know how he went away to Vietnam and came back a different man, and how it took him two years to pick up a gun again. I also wasn't supposed to know how Mama got pregnant before she married my daddy and how all they did was fight until he left one rainy night on his motorcycle and got killed on the highway. I never met my daddy, but that was the story I wish I hadn't heard. I learned a lot about grownup things back then because I was always the quietest in the room. I suppose people talk more when they don't know who's listening.

The day after the preacher visited our house, Albert goaded me on the railroad tracks. "You're such a scare baby. Just go put your toe in the Shiloh creek and come back."

"Why don't you do it?"

"Because I told you to first. If you do it, I'll give you my railroad penny." He couldn't have told me anything more tempting than that. His penny fascinated me. Albert had placed it on the tracks and the train ran over it. All that pressure from the heavy train and the penny didn't break. It just changed shape. I wanted that penny, but I didn't like Shiloh. Even Onnie warned me away from that place.

Albert held up the coin, tempting me to answer his dare. My pride tempted me more than that old railroad penny. I looked down the tracks in the direction of Shiloh.

"You'd better not," Sam said. "Albert, don't let her. You know we'll get our rear ends busted for this one." His black hair fell over his eye, and he blew it away.

"Not if you don't tell." Albert spit on the railroad tracks, his way of marking his territory and asserting his authority. It worked. Sam didn't object.

I started walking. The gravel between the ties crunched underneath my sneakers and sweat trickled down my neck under the hair that had fallen loose from my ponytail. The sun beamed down on the tracks so hot that if you looked where they followed, the heat bent the air. Spotting a railroad spike, I picked it up. You never passed up a loose railroad spike on the tracks. I turned it over in my hands and noticed it curved in the middle, so I threw it down and wiped the rust from my hands. Spotting another, I bent over to retrieve it.

"Stop stalling! Are you going or not?"

"I'm going!"

All I had to do was put my toe in the creek. The creek was a good way past the shack houses so maybe I could get in and out without being spotted. The houses were on a slope, parallel to the railroad tracks in front, and to the creek in the back. Sometimes you could see women washing clothes in the creek while their kids splashed around in the water. I approached the neighborhood from the far-right side, making my way toward the creek. One, two, three rows of houses later, I still hadn't seen anyone, so I started for the water.

"What are you doing here?" A hand jerked my arm. I looked up into the ugliest face I had ever seen. Screaming, I squirmed and wiggled to get away, but he held me tight. "I asked you a question. What are you doing here? You don't belong here, girl, and maybe someone needs to teach you a lesson, sneaking around black folks' homes where you don't belong."

"Cecil Farley, you let her go. Now." I knew that voice.

The man turned and snarled. "Well, look a here. If it ain't my old woman. What are you doing here, Onnie?"

"I ain't going to tell you twice, Cecil. Put her down." She raised a pistol and aimed it at his head.

The man cursed and released me. I ran to Onnie's side. "Get behind me, girl."

"Now, Onnie. You won't shoot me."

"I'll do what I have to do. Just like last time."

He visibly winced. I finally took a good look at the man's face and shrunk at the horror of it. His scarred cheek made Onnie's scar look like a scratch. His skin was a wrinkled mass of tissue, with folds of disfigured flesh that enveloped his eye and extended to his ear.

"I know what you did last time, Onnie. I haven't forgotten." He rubbed his ugly cheek.

"Is that a threat in your voice, Cecil? While I'm pointing a loaded pistol at you?"

"You won't always have a pistol."

"We both know you've hurt me all you're going to in this life, Cecil, and you won't hurt this here child, neither."

She backed away and pulled me with her. She didn't take her eyes or the gun off the man until we had reached the tracks. My cousins had disappeared from sight.

Onnie wasted no time lighting into me. "What in tarnation were you doing at Shiloh, girl?"

"I—"

"Oh, I know. I heard the whole thing. When I saw you walking with those boys this way, I followed. And it's a good thing I did, too. Ain't you got no common sense, child?"

My mama said that to me all the time. I picked up my pace and got ahead of her.

"Hold it."

I stopped and slowly turned around.

"You ain't getting off that easy. You could at least keep a woman company for a bit after she rescued you from the likes of Cecil Farley.

"But my cousins..."

"Your cousins done left you to fend for yourself. I don't think you need to worry about them none. At least not right now." She grasped my hand and led me to her house. As we approached Color Town, several pairs of dark eyes followed us down the street. She sang a song I had never heard before. "His eye is on the sparrow, and I know He watches me." I liked the sound of her smooth, low tones.

Once inside her house, I felt safe enough to ask. "Who was that man, Onnie?"

"That man is a bad man and that is all you need to know."

"He hurt you, didn't he?" I pointed to her face.

She walked over to her dining table and started folding towels. "Yes."

"And you hurt him?"

She stopped and looked at me. "You're a keen little thing, aren't you?"

"What's keen?"

"It means you can see more than most. Only thing is, that usually means you've seen more than you should." I figured Onnie was keen, too.

"What was that song you were singing on the street?"

"It's an old hymn my mama taught me years ago. She used to sing me to sleep with the old gospel hymns. There was nothing quite so fine as my mama's voice."

"You must take after her because you have a fine voice, too."

"Thank you. Maybe next time you can sing with me."

"I don't know that song."

"Ah. Well, I can teach you. Can you figure out what it means?" She asked, watching my face as she stacked the towels together in the laundry basket.

"I don't know. Is it about God?"

"Yes, it is about God. And us."

"But what about the bird? Isn't it also about a bird?"

She laughed. "Yes, it's about a bird, but only to get a point across to us humans."

I frowned. "I don't get it."

"Yes, you do. A keen little girl like you. Think it over while you help." She tossed me a towel. I picked up the corners and made the ends meet, then I dropped it in front of me.

"If He watches out for the little birds, He can watch out for us, too. Right?"

She smiled. "That's right."

She started singing again, and this time I tried singing along with her, but in the back of my mind a thought nagged at me like a fly on a mule. If God watched out for Onnie, then why did she get such a nasty scar? And if He watched out for me, then why did I have to be so afraid to go home?

I was right to be afraid that night because Mama waited for me. Albert and Sam had told her where I'd gone.

"You know you're not supposed to go near Shiloh! Or Color Town! Why were you there?"

"Albert told me to..."

"I don't care what Albert told you to do, you don't belong around those ——."

She said a word that I knew wasn't a nice word. A word that didn't belong to Onnie. She got the belt out of her bedroom; the one daddy had left the night he walked out. She pushed me violently to my bedroom and shoved me onto my bed. The first few lashes stung but were bearable. It was always after the fifth or sixth that had me begging God to let me die.

Once Mama got started, she couldn't stop. I always knew when her rage cloaked her mind. The pain forced me to cry out, which enraged her further, so she swung the belt onto my neck, back, thighs and legs, as well as my backside. She swung and swung until her rage transferred to me. I didn't know it then, but my tears were full of it.

The following morning, there were no pancakes. I didn't see Mama all that day. The cigarette smoke coming from her room made me cough, but I stifled it with my arm so I wouldn't disturb her. I didn't dare leave the house, even though I never saw her. For breakfast, I had cereal, and for lunch, I had a sandwich made of bread and peanut butter. There was no jelly. I looked in the refrigerator at dinnertime and found eggs, so I gently pulled a chair up to the stove and scrambled some. I made a little noise, but she never came out of her room. After washing my dishes, I went to my own room and climbed into bed.

I wanted to see Onnie. She had never physically embraced me, but that night I dreamed of sitting on her lap as she brushed my hair and she sang, "His Eye is on the Sparrow".

The next day, Mama and I went to church. We sang the exact song that Onnie sang on the street and in my dream. It sounded different than how Onnie sang it. It was even hotter than the day before, but I wore long sleeves and Mama didn't put my hair in a ponytail. The preacher spoke about forgiveness. He said something about forgiving someone seventy times seven.

He said we are to forgive over and over even when we are hurt over and over.

On my notepad, I drew a stick woman with a scar on her face holding a child with scribbles on her arms and legs. Both were crying.

# 3

"We told on you because we were scared." Sam said, his red lips and tongue making his lie that much more ridiculous.

We sat on the back porch at Mamaw's, sucking on popsicles she made from Kool-Aid with her Tupperware popsicle kit. The popsicles were much fatter than the store-bought kind, but once you sucked on them for a minute, the Kool-Aid disappeared, and you were left with ice. Still, it cooled us off.

"Who was that woman? The one that helped you?" Albert asked. He wore his favorite cap; the one Uncle Brody gave him that had the Holder's logo on it.

"Shhhh!" I said. I could hear Mamaw in the kitchen because the screen door was open. "I don't know. She just helped me. Besides, I wouldn't have needed help if you hadn't made me go there in the first place."

"I didn't make you go there. You could have said no." He bit a big chunk of ice and spit it at Sam. Sam picked it up and threw it at me. I dodged it.

"Well, anyway, I did, so you owe me your flattened railroad penny."

"I don't owe you anything. The deal was for you to stick your toe in the water. You didn't, so no penny." This time he spat a piece of ice on the ground.

I knew technically he was right, but something in me just felt like I deserved that penny after all I went through that day. I threw down my popsicle, balled my fists and drew back. Before I could swing at him, Albert pushed me off the porch to the ground. He jumped on top of me and held me down.

"Albert, you can't hit no girl." Sam protested.

"I'll hit her if she hits me first!"

I bit him on the arm. He yelped and let go of my arms long enough for me to punch him in the face. He plopped down on the grass, holding his nose. Blood poured over his lips and down his chin. I jumped on top of him.

"Tara, if you don't stop, I'll tell Mamaw about your colored friend." Sam yelled.

"You'll tell me about her what?" Mamaw stood at the back door, hands on her hips. She frowned at us.

I released Albert. Mamaw curled her finger at me the way she always did when she wanted me to come to her. I resisted the urge to punch Albert's smug, Kool-Aid and blood- stained face. I walked up the porch to the back door, then followed her inside. The screen door slammed shut behind me. She went back to the table and picked up a tomato from a large bowl of ice water and began peeling it with a paring knife. I had seen her peel tomatoes like this before. She always boiled them first, then put them in the ice water to make the skins easier to come off. Her apron looked like it belonged on a horror film set, with the red juices splattered all over the front of it.

I walked over to the sink to grab the old, dented cup Mamaw had attached to a wire on the cabinet. We all drank from that cup and thought nothing of it then. The water tasted so good and cold from that old cup.

"You gonna tell me what they're talking about or am I gonna have to go get my switch?"

Mamaw always threatened to get her switch, but she had never used it on me. I had seen her use it on Albert once. He needed to see that switch more often the way I saw it. If only Mamaw hadn't come outside when she did. I could've given Albert the pounding he deserved.

"Well?"

"A colored lady helped me, is all." I picked up a tomato and rubbed its smooth skin.

"What colored lady? Helped you do what?"

"I was at Shiloh—"

Mamaw dropped her knife. "Shiloh! Land's sakes, girl, what were you doing there? You know better than that. I ought to get my switch anyway."

"I already got punished by Mama." I rolled a tomato around on top of the table, so I didn't have to meet her eyes. She stared at me a moment, then went back to her tomatoes.

A few moments of silence passed as I watched her work the knife under the skin of the tomato, then pull it off in strips. She sighed and set her knife down again before looking at me.

"Why don't you help me in here for a bit?" She went to a drawer and pulled out another apron, helping me tie it around my waist. She rarely let anyone help her in the kitchen.

"What about Albert's nose?"

"I suppose he can manage just fine. If not, we can charge him a flattened railroad penny for the price of a tissue."

We both giggled at that. She didn't ask about Onnie again. I was glad. I loved Mamaw Webb, but I wasn't ready to tell her about Onnie yet. Besides, although I had seen Mamaw talk friendly with black ladies in the grocery store, I had never seen her peel tomatoes with them in her kitchen.

———

Church became a bit more pleasant for me the following weeks. We had started going three times a week and I made a friend in Sunday school. I found out Cindy lived right up the road past my grandparent's house, in the back of the service station. Her daddy owned the service station so she, her mama, her baby sister, and her daddy lived in the back. She told me her daddy had turned it into living quarters to save money. Mama said she couldn't imagine such a thing, living in a store, but I thought it was fabulous. Cindy brought me a treat every Sunday from the store. Sometimes it was colorful gum, with the zebra on the package, and other times it was those red ball shaped candies that burned my mouth. They were my favorites. I wasn't allowed to have either in church, so I usually stuck it in my pocket for later.

Cindy didn't mean to, but she got me into trouble with her treats one Sunday. Her mama had allowed her to sit with me. Sometimes they missed Sunday school because they were helping with the store.

"I didn't forget your treat." She whispered after the sermon started.

"You don't have to bring me something every Sunday." I told her, although I looked forward to it every week.

"It's okay. My dad doesn't mind. Here." She held out her hand. I reached for the candy and gasped.

"Cigarettes!" I whispered.

She giggled. "No, silly. These are candy cigarettes. They're just pretend."

"Shhhh!" I looked up to see my mama's firm stare. I shoved the candy into my little purse, but I couldn't listen to the sermon. I was too distracted by the idea of those candy cigarettes.

Every week after the service, we had to go through the "enjoyed it" line, as I called it. The "enjoyed it" line was when we all shook the preacher's hand and told him we enjoyed his sermon. My mama always took a long time in this line. It reminded me of when Jimmy Peterson lingered over the water fountain at school and Mrs. Foster had to shoo him away so the rest of us could have a turn. There was no Mrs. Foster to shoo my mama away from the preacher.

But there were candy cigarettes. Candy cigarettes that fell out of my purse, rolled out of their package, and landed right at the preacher's feet. That moment changed how I looked at the preacher because that's when I really saw Reverend Martin's eyes for the first time. Eyes that said he didn't like candy cigarettes.

The next day, I heard a voice in our kitchen when I walked up to the back door.

"I believe she's a bad influence on Tara." Reverend Martin said.

What was he doing here? The smell of coffee told me he'd already been here a while. I knew I shouldn't have, but I stood to the side of the screen door, listening.

"She needs a friend, Reverend. I just thought—"

"You need to be careful who she hangs around. They live in a service station, Ellie, where they sell real cigarettes and beer." Did he not know my mama smoked? And I had never heard him call her by her first name before.

"But they get along so well. She finally has a girl to play with instead of those rowdy cousins of hers. I thought it'd be good for her."

"Well, you just think on it. Anyway, at least they come to church some." I heard the scrape of the chair on the floor.

I peeked in and saw Reverend Martin standing close to my mama. He patted her arm and said goodbye. She stood there for a while, staring off after him. I'd seen that look before. My stomach burned sick at what that look meant. Reverend Martin's wife taught me Sunday school at church. She played the piano, too, and I liked how she swayed and closed her eyes as she played, as if she forgot everything around her but the music. When she spoke, she had the softest voice. I liked her. I didn't want Mama to change Ms. Martin's voice.

Cindy never came to church on Sunday nights because that was a busy night at her dad's store. I dreaded Sunday night services because I was the only girl my age that came. Most of the people who showed up on Sunday nights were older people, or they had little kids who acted up so much their mamas had to take them out of the service. When they came back to their pews, the kids always had red eyes and hiccups from crying so I tried not to look at them. One Sunday night before church, a man with glasses and a beard shook my hand and winked at me. He asked me my name and then he showed me a trick with his thumb. I didn't dare to tell him that it was a baby trick, especially with my mama watching. He redeemed himself for mistaking me for a baby when he told me to hold out my hand. He dropped a bunch of butterscotch into my palm and winked.

"Sweets for the sweet." he said. Every Sunday night he gave me candy. On Sunday mornings he gave both Cindy and me butterscotch and Tootsie Rolls. We started calling him The Candy Man.

Besides him and Mrs. Martin, I liked a few others. There was Mrs. Templeton, who wore a sweater no matter how hot the day was, and it almost always had cat hair on it. She cackled so loud whenever she heard something funny. Even if I didn't know what she laughed at, I laughed with her, and so did everybody else. There was Bob, the man that cleaned the church after services. If we stayed too long talking, he'd flash the lights up and down to get us to leave. Or, when he vacuumed, he'd place the hose on our heads and suck up our hair while we giggled and screamed. He also took up the offering and once when I placed a dollar bill in the plate, he took it out and put it into his pocket, before laughing and putting it back. Then there was Mrs. Gibson. Mrs. Gibson wasn't really that pretty, but she always dressed like she was, with makeup, jewelry, and the fanciest dresses. She had shiny, red hair and wore it in a pixie cut. She sang "specials" every Sunday. Mama said they ought to let someone else have a turn, but I didn't care. Mrs. Gibson sang like Patsy Cline, strong, but smooth, and she made me want to listen to her for hours. She and Onnie would have sounded great together in a duet. Still, The Candy Man took the lead in my group of favorite church people. Not just because he gave me candy, but because he complimented me every time he saw me. He told me how pretty my eyes were, and that I could be a professional artist one day when he looked at my pictures on my notebook. He had no idea that I would have traded all the butterscotch and tootsie rolls in the world just to hear him say nice things to me every Sunday. Or maybe he did.

# 4

Mama still let me play with Cindy. I couldn't forget what the preacher said, though, and it kind of spoiled the time I had playing with her. I loved going to her house at the service station. Her parents didn't speak to me much. We played while they worked. Her little sister sat in a playpen inside the store so Cindy and I either played Connect Four or Battleship, or we roamed around outside on the streets or through the cotton fields. Sometimes we helped stock shelves in the store, which I thought was a fun thing to do. Cindy didn't like it. I figured it was much like the time I first helped Mamaw snap beans. I liked it until I had to do it several times. Cindy's apartment in the back of the gas station only had three rooms and a bathroom. One large room had a sofa and love seat. The kitchen was also a part of that room. Cindy had to share her room with her baby sister, so the crib took up most of her toy space. Her parent's room had a bunch of boxes piled in one corner.

"My daddy says this is temporary. We're going to get another house." Cindy said one day. We were on her bed, taking turns looking through reels on her red View-Master of castles in Europe.

"I think it's cool that you live here. You can have candy and soda anytime you want."

"Well, not anytime I want. Daddy still has to pay for them, you know."

"Right." I hadn't thought of that.

"What about you? Do you get to have all the cotton you want?"

"What do you mean?" I asked.

"You know, your grandfather's farm. You can just go pick cotton anytime."

"Yeah, but what would I want to do that for? I mean it's nice and all, but there's not much you can do with it except hold it and rub it on your face, and even then, it's not that soft because of the seeds."

"Oh. Right. Well, what about cotton candy?"

"Cotton candy?" I gave her a confused stare. She rolled her eyes.

"Tara, don't you know that you can make cotton candy?"

"Out of real cotton?"

"Of course. How else would they make it?"

"But I don't know how."

"It can't be that hard. We just need a little food coloring and sugar. And we'll have to pick cotton, of course, and get the seeds out. I guess that part's hard."

"I don't know..." It seemed a bit far-fetched to me. "Why doesn't my Mamaw make it? She makes everything."

"Maybe she doesn't know how, either, or maybe she just doesn't have time to pick out all the seeds."

"Maybe. But I still think they would have told me."

"Well, maybe they didn't want you taking all the cotton for the cotton candy."

"That makes sense." I nodded.

"Well, let's go." She jumped up from her bed.

We picked the soft, white bolls until our fingers hurt. When we filled a brown paper sack we brought from the store, we took them back to her house and laid them out on the kitchen table. We spent a good part of the day, pulling at the seeds and trying to keep too much cotton from sticking to them.

"Why is it so thick? Seems like cotton candy is thinner."

"Maybe we have to stretch it out before we stir in the coloring and sugar. Okay, you do that while I find the food coloring. What color do we want?" She rummaged through a cabinet above the stove.

"Blue." I said, pulling at the cotton.

She came back and we poured sugar and food coloring in a bowl and mixed in the cotton. It didn't look like the cotton candy at the fair.

"I bet we have to have a machine or something.' I said.

"Well, let's taste it. I bet it tastes good anyway."

I pulled at a sticky piece and tentatively placed it on my tongue. Cindy did the same. It did not dissolve like regular cotton candy. We looked at each other, jumped up, and raced for the garbage can to spit it out. Cupping our hands, we flushed our tongues with tap water. Then, we laughed until our sides ached.

"You'd better not tell anyone about this." Cindy said.

"I won't. It'll be our funny secret."

"That's what friends are for. Telling secrets."

I had so much fun that day, I forgot about what the preacher said to Mama about Cindy. I didn't tell her that secret. I didn't tell her about Onnie, either. Only Albert, Sam, and Mamaw knew anything about her, and even they thought she was just a kind stranger to me. Truth is, I had been seeing Onnie every Wednesday, the morning after Mama's night shift at the sewing factory. She always slept a lot during that day, so she didn't miss me.

Wednesday was my favorite day. I got to see Onnie during the day, then Cindy at church on Wednesday night. Although we had to sit quietly for the preaching, we often found ways to communicate.

What happened to your arm? Cindy wrote in tiny letters on a gum wrapper. I had become accustomed to reading her messages this way. She passed it to me, along with her pen.

I fell out of a tree. I wrote back. She frowned, looking at my arm.

But that looks like finger marks.

I thought quickly. My cousin tried to grab me so I wouldn't fall. I almost ran out of room on the gum wrapper. Cindy nodded and stopped writing since it was time for the invitation when folks went down to the carpeted steps, or altar, to pray. We all stood with our hymnals, singing "I Surrender All" while Reverend Martin asked if anyone wanted to come to the altar to pray for repentance and forgiveness.

I almost walked down. Because I had just lied in church.

---

"Onnie, do you go to church?" I asked her one day while we drank lemonade on her porch.

"As a matter of fact, I do. Why?"

"We started going to church. I don't like it; except I do like seeing my friend Cindy. And there are some other nice people, too."

"Well, then why don't you like it?"

I shrugged. "I don't know."

"Yes, you do. Don't be shrugging your shoulders about important stuff. Save that for things that don't matter."

"You think church matters?"

"Don't you?"

"I know my Mamaw does. She always wanted my mama to take me to her church, but Mama never wanted to go. Until now."

"Oh? Why is that?"

"She likes the preacher at this church."

"Ah. Well, I tell ya, child, church matters. But not because people expect good people to go, or because we like certain people there. We're all bad, you know. And we're all needing church."

"Because we sin?"

She laughed. "Yes, because we sin. But we need each other, too. First, we need what the Good Lord did for us, then we need what we can do for each other."

"I suppose. I'm glad I see Cindy there."

"That's good. You need a friend."

"You're my friend, Onnie."

She stopped and her eyes teared up. "Yes, I am, and you're mine. Since I'm your friend, I have a question."

"What?"

"Does your daddy know?"

"Know what?"

"That your mama hits you."

I looked down at my lemonade. A gnat had flown into it. I swirled my glass around and watched it struggle.

"Tara, friends don't lie to friends."

"My daddy died. But she doesn't do it all the time. She just has a hard time with her job and stuff."

"There ain't no excuses for anyone hurtin' a child. Don't make 'em for her. It won't do you no good, nor her neither. I'm also not suggesting you be angry with her. That won't do any more good than making excuses. And stop making assumptions about why she's doing it. Assumptions are like eatin' the bread before it's done. So often lies are just our own truths that go untested. One of these days you're gonna have to test it."

Talking to Onnie about my mama brought the butterfly ache to my stomach. I loved Onnie, and I knew she loved me, but it didn't feel right. I wanted to take it back and tell her I really did fall, and that Mama had never hit me. It was too late. Onnie would always know the secret about mama. Once you know something, you just can't un-know it. Kinda like knowing what a boll of cotton tasted like.

"You know what we can do?" She asked.

"What?"

"We can have a secret exchange."

"What's a secret exchange?"

"It's where friends swap secrets. You already told me one, now I'll tell you one."

I perked up, thinking any secret Onnie had must be good.

"Okay, here goes. I used to get hit, too." Any excitement I had died with that statement.

"Is that how you got that scar?" I pointed to her cheek.

"Yes, it is. Do you remember Cecil?"

I nodded but didn't tell her I couldn't forget him since he'd been in my nightmares so many nights since I went to Shiloh.

"Well, we used to be married."

I had seen in cartoons where jaws dropped to the ground, and I felt like mine looked just like that then. I couldn't imagine Onnie being married to that scary, ugly man.

"I made excuses for Cecil for years. Then, when I found out just how horrible he was, I decided I was done making excuses. But that's enough secret telling. How about we take these glasses inside and I can show you how to make buttermilk biscuits and gravy."

Onnie didn't ask me anymore about my bruises or my mama and I didn't ask her about her scar. As we rolled the rolling pin over the dough, I told her about Albert's bloody nose and how Mamaw said he could pay for the tissue with the railroad penny he owed me.

Onnie laughed aloud and said, "More folks ought to pay for their tissues when it's their own fault they need 'em."

# 5

Church potluck in the south was a religion on its own. Baptists knew how to throw a fellowship meal together and make it seem as spiritual an experience as the sermon itself. For my first Baptist potluck, Mama and I brought chips and dip, and little chicken salad sandwiches cut into round shapes. There was fried chicken, potato salad, cornbread, baked beans, casseroles of all kinds, and the dessert table, which was filled with apple pie, cookies, and cakes. Our little church only had about 30 members, including Mama and me, but the food still disappeared.

Cindy didn't come that night, so I was the only girl my age there. There had been a gospel singing with a family group of two brothers and a sister. One played guitar, one played the drums, and the sister played the keyboard. She had feathered hair like that lady on Charlie's Angels, only she wasn't quite as pretty. They all sang, but I didn't like the lady's voice, which was raspy and shook with too much vibrato. After the singing, we got to eat, but that didn't last too long, and I got bored while the adults talked. Outside, the kids played on the playground. I didn't want to play with little kids, so I went back to my Sunday school room to color. Finding some pink construction paper and safety scissors, I made a card for Onnie that had a cut out bird glued on it. She liked birds.

The corner of my eye caught movement. The Candy Man stood at the door. He smiled at me and came over to the table.

"Why aren't you playing outside with the other kids?"

"I don't know. They're just little. I don't want to play what they play."

"I understand. What's this?" He took the card from me. "Who's Onnie?"

"She's just a friend. She doesn't go here. She goes to another church." I didn't lie.

"That's a pretty card. Your friend will love it. I told you how good your art is, didn't I?" He put the card back on the table and moved closer. I could hear the group in the front of the church warming up for their next session.

"My mama might be looking for me. I'd better go see." I moved to get up from the chair.

He nudged me back to my seat. "No, they're just practicing. It will be a little while. Everybody's still eating, and your mama is busy talking. Why don't you sit and talk with me a bit?" He unwrapped a butterscotch and put it to my mouth. I opened wide and let him put it in.

"Thank you." The candy didn't mix well with the sour cream and onion taste on my tongue.

I wondered why he didn't want to talk to the adults, but he was nice and seemed to like me, so I stayed. Mama couldn't get mad at me if an adult said it was okay. We colored on some of the extra Bible color sheets, and he told me all about his dog. I had always wanted a dog. His told me how his dog chewed his shoes and got into a fight with a skunk last year.

"He covered his own nose with his paws for days after that."

I giggled at that mental picture. He put his arm around me and pulled me close. It felt nice to be hugged. Then, he kissed my cheek. I didn't really like that because his beard scraped my skin and his breath smelled like turnip greens.

He got up and I thought he was leaving, but he closed the door and shut off the light. I got up to leave, thinking we'd go join the others, but he pulled me to him. The group started to sing, and I could hear the lady's raspy voice, but soon my soft crying would drown them out. I never ate butterscotch candy again.

I walked back to the fellowship hall. Mama stood there with the pastor, laughing, and touching his arm. I had already thrown up in the bathroom, but my stomach threatened to vomit again. The Candy man sat with his wife when I walked in. He didn't look at me but ate the chips and the sour cream and onion dip we brought.

"Mama, can we go home? I don't feel so good."

"What? Oh, Tara, why now? The group's going to sing again. You know I've been looking forward to this all week."

"Ellie, if she's sick, surely you want to take her home." Ms. Martin spoke softly, but firmly. Both curiosity and sympathy shined in her eyes.

My mama sighed in annoyance. Mrs. Martin frowned, then watched her husband who watched Mama.

"I'll take her to the nursery, and she can lie down there." Mama said, grabbing my hand abruptly.

Mrs. Martin stood. "You know what? I'm not feeling so well myself. I'll take her to the parsonage out back and when service is over, you can pick her up."

"You're going to miss the rest of the service?" Reverend Martin scowled.

"Like I said, I'm not feeling well. I'm sure no one will mind if I'm gone." Her voice sounded funny. She touched me gently and guided me outside.

I wanted Mama to change her mind. I wanted her to get me as far away from that place as possible. But she didn't even say a word to me as I walked out with Mrs. Martin. She was too busy laughing at something Reverend Martin said. There was someone watching me, though. The Candy man smiled and waved to me as I followed Mrs. Martin outside.

As soon as we reached the parsonage, I ran to the bathroom and threw up again.

"I'm telling you we can reach the devil if we dig far enough."
Albert said.

"You're crazy."

"Sam, tell her it's true."

"It's true. Hell is under the earth. Satan's there."

"And what do we do if we find him? We're just kids."

"We can take him. All we have to do is shout Jesus at him and
then he'll be weak. Everybody knows Satan can't stand Jesus'
name. Once he's weak, we take these here shovels and we hit
him. Just think. We kill the devil and there'll be no more evil. We
kill the devil, and everyone will love us." He sounded so sure, but
I felt the same uncertainty I felt with Cindy when she wanted
to make cotton candy. Still, I took a shovel and dug.

Since it had just rained, the shovels sunk into the dirt with
ease. My arms hurt after only a few minutes of digging, and
Sam had already sat down. Albert attacked the chore with
steady exuberance like he always did on one of his missions.

"Look! I told you!" he yelled.

"What?" Sam and I yelled back.

"Right there! That's red dirt! We're getting closer to Hell!"

Sam threw a clump of clay at him. "Oh, Albert, there's red
dirt everywhere. That don't mean nothing. We're going to get in
so much trouble for digging in Papaw's field.

"Nah, he won't care. There's no cotton planted right here." I
said. "Hey, Albert, why do you want to find the devil and kill
him?"

"I don't know. Because it's cool. Besides, if the devil's dead, my
daddy won't drink anymore."

I looked at Sam and he looked back at me. We both got up
and started digging again. An hour later, bugs blinked light all
around us. We never called them fireflies but lightening bugs.
We threw down our shovels and ran to get some jars from
Mamaw. After poking holes in the lids, we caught some of the
blinking bugs and then screwed the lid back on. Then, we sat in
that deep hole we dug and just admired the shiny little lights.

"Do you really think we could have found the devil down there?" Sam asked his brother.

"Naw. I guess I just wanted to pretend. You know, like when Papaw pretends not to believe in God."

"Papaw believes in God?" I asked.

"Yeah. All that talk about church is just to look tough. I catch him reading his Bible sometimes."

"I wonder why he won't go to church with us." Sam said.

"I think he just got mad at the hypocrites."

"What's a hypocrite?" I asked.

"It's when folks act like they doing something when they ain't. You know like when Sam acts like he's trying to be good but really, he just don't want to get in trouble. He's a hypocrite."

Sam's face turned red. He put down his jar of lightening bugs and jumped at Albert. He punched and punched, but Albert just giggled and yelled, "Stop, Sam! The bugs!"

I grabbed the jars of bugs and went toward the house. If I hurried, I could get use of the washtub first. Mamaw never let us use her bathtub in the house after getting so dirty. Instead, we had to take turns using the big washtub on her back porch. The first one in had the cleanest water.

"What in Sam Hill were ya'll doing out there? You look like a little colored girl." Mamaw said. She poured some hot water in with me as I scrubbed my head clean.

"We were digging to Hell."

"What?" She stopped pouring and looked at me.

"Digging to Hell. Albert said we could kill the devil if we dug down to Hell."

"Land's sakes. You kids ain't got the sense God gave a billy goat."

"You don't think we could dig to Hell?"

"Tara Gail, I think you three have enough devils in your own minds that you need to kill before you start looking for 'em in Hell. And no, you need to leave the devil to Jesus. He'll get him when the time's right." She shook her head and laughed as she walked back into the house.

I thought about Uncle Brody's drinking. I thought about butterscotch candy and long-sleeved shirts in the summertime. I thought about Onnie's scar. Mamaw was right. We didn't have to go to Hell to find the devil.

# 6

I never told anyone about the Candy Man. Not even Onnie. He still gave me candy at church in front of everyone, so I had to accept it. I never ate it, though, and I never left the adults again during any fellowship dinners.

In the middle of July, I had just come home from playing outside at Mamaw's house with Cindy, Albert, and Sam. We had built a fort in the front yard with branches that Papaw had cut from his fruit trees. Cindy came over often since she lived just up the road. I liked when she played with us because Albert didn't boss me around as much.

We all knew to go home when it got dusk. That's when the mosquito truck would pass through and spray the poisonous fog we weren't supposed to breathe. It would drive slowly around the main roads and some of the back roads, too, releasing a cloud of pesticide that lingered long enough to ruin our playtime. By the time it dissipated, it was dark, and we could only be outside after dark in our own yards. It always seemed to happen when we were having the most fun.

I saw Reverend Martin's car parked in our driveway. It wasn't unusual on a Saturday. That's when he often made his visits, and sometimes Mrs. Martin accompanied him. I got excited to see her, so I ran to the side of the house to the water spigot to wash my face. She always inspired me to look presentable. I was a tomboy, but I figured when I was old enough, I'd be sure to act like Mrs. Martin. It wasn't so much in how she dressed, but how she behaved. Mrs. Martin reminded me of those ladies in the old movies that wore gloves on their hands, and pearls on their necks while they sipped hot tea.

When I walked into the house, the lights were off. I heard something in Mama's bedroom and went to investigate. I looked through the cracked door and almost fell backwards with shock. I quietly backed out of the hallway and then ran out the back door.

I could only think of one place to go. I ran through the cloud of bug spray, arriving at Onnie's house, coughing, and sputtering. If I died, at least Onnie would be with me.

"Lord, have mercy, child, what are you doing on the streets with that poison floatin' around? Get in this house!" She swung open the screen door.

I threw myself at her and began to sob. She spoke in soothing tones as she stroked my hair. Her apron smelled so familiar, like Pine Sol and fried chicken. She let me cry for a spell, then told me to sit down at the table.

After eating a plate of fried chicken, mashed potatoes, green beans, and cornbread, I swallowed down the rest of my iced tea while Onnie watched me.

"Are you going to tell me why you're here, and why you were crying?"

I shook my head. "I can't."

"Did she hit you again?" I shook my head no.

"Alright, I won't force you, but I know your mama is probably looking for you, and it won't do you no good for her to find out you've been here."

She was right, but I didn't want to leave. I didn't want to go back and see any more of what I saw. I didn't want to be back in that house.

"Of course, I can't let you walk back by yourself, so I guess she'll find out anyway."

I stood up from the table. "No! You can't! I can go by myself."

"Tara, do you remember the day I got you away from Cecil?"

"Yes."

"Well, there's plenty more where he comes from, roaming around out there, and even worse than his kind." A face flashed before my mind. The memory scent of butterscotch candy threatened to make me gag. Onnie didn't notice my inner struggle.

"Now, let's clear our plates and head out. I don't own a car, so we'll have to walk."

She had that tone that said it was futile to argue, but she had no idea that the dark road home wasn't what scared me. It was home itself.

Onnie decided to stay a distance away from my house so I could arrive alone. I turned to look at her again before I opened my front door, but she had already turned around to go home. Resisting the urge to follow her, I opened the door.

"Where have you been?" Mama yelled and grabbed me by the arm. I winced with the pinch of her grip. I could smell his cologne on her.

"I didn't realize it was so late. I was playing."

"I called your Mamaw's house an hour ago. You weren't there! Your cousins were already eating supper."

"I got distracted. I wanted to catch a frog on the road."

"Tara Gail, I know when you're lying to me." She slapped me across the face. I brought my elbows up to guard against another slap. Too late. Her hand caught my lip.

What could I say? I was lying. I wanted to ask her why it was wrong when I did it, but it wasn't wrong for her or even the preacher.

"Why do you smell like chicken?" she asked. I stared in fear. I hadn't thought about hiding the smell of Onnie's supper.

"I don't know." My voice quivered and I swallowed to control it. My fear only fed her anger.

She slapped me across the face again. "Don't lie to me!" She cursed and called me a name I wasn't supposed to say, ever.

"That's what you are!" I suddenly screamed out. "I saw you! I saw you with him in your bedroom!" The scream scratched my throat.

Her eyes hardened, then looked wild and furious. Grabbing me by my hair, she pulled me to her bedroom and shoved me on her bed. She pulled my pants down before grabbing the belt from her drawer. Over and over the belt came down on my bare flesh. Raw pain seared my back and legs until I thought I couldn't bear it anymore. I heard a strange sound, then realized it was my strangled cry underneath the pressure of her hand on my head, forcing my face onto the bedspread. I prayed she'd just kill me and get it over with.

When she finally finished punishing me for her sins, she walked out and slammed the door. I heard the engine to her car start outside.

I went into the bathroom and soothed my raw, stinging flesh with warm bath water. My only thought as I dried off was that it was a good thing the whelps were only on my upper thighs this time so I could still wear my favorite shorts instead of blue jeans.

The next day, Reverend Martin preached on being a hypocrite. Mama held her Bible open in her lap. I couldn't look at Mrs. Martin. I'd almost rather look at the Candy Man. Almost.

---

Onnie didn't ask me what happened when I got home, but I think she knew.

"We're going to have a chef's day today."

"A what?" I asked her.

"A chef's day. I'm going to start teaching you all my recipes. Even the Cajun ones Cecil taught me before he turned so mean. He was quite the cook in his day. His mama was a cook on a captain's boat out of New Orleans. She taught him how to prepare all kinds of spicy, rich foods. And he taught me. Now I'm going to teach you. That is, if you want to learn. You seemed to enjoy learning how to make biscuits the other day."

"I loved it! Mamaw sometimes lets me help her in the kitchen, but not much since I'm so little."

"Little's got nothin' to do with it. It's the want to in a person that makes a being capable. And I think you have plenty of want to. Don't you?"

"Yes, ma'am." She started absently singing while pulling out spices and ingredients. "Onnie, what's that song?"

"Huh? Oh. It's what called a black spiritual song. It's called 'Deep River'."

"It's so pretty."

"Do you want to learn it?"

I nodded yes. I wondered how it'd sound coming from Mrs. Gibson's voice.

Later, as we cooked, she told all about New Orleans and how Cecil took her to visit there. She described the city with colorful images in her words. That day with Onnie I discovered two things. One, Onnie often complimented me, but not like The Candy Man. She complimented me by entrusting me to do things. And two, I knew what I wanted to be when I grew up. A Cajun chef in a fancy New Orleans restaurant.

# 7

S ounds came from Onnie's house as I walked up the steps to the porch. I looked through the screen door and saw a boy sitting on the sofa watching TV. He didn't notice me yet. He had on one of those hats that the boy on Oliver Twist wore. At the kitchen table, a woman sat with Onnie. She wore a colorful blue and yellow pants suit with gold bangled bracelets up one arm. Large, hooped earrings dangled from her ears. She was pretty. It shocked me that I thought that. I had never really looked at black people as pretty or ugly. They were just black. Maybe it was because I had never known a black person before, up close. Onnie stood out to me because she had a scar. I mentally corrected myself. That wasn't true. There were many things about Onnie that stood out.

"I just need you to watch him for me for a couple of weeks, Onnie. That's all. I'll come back and get 'em as soon as I have a job and I'm all settled."

"Clarissa, last time you didn't come back for two months. That boy don't want to stay here with me."

"It's just 'cause he ain't really your grandkid and you don't want to fool with him."

"You know that's not true. I love you like you was my own, and that there boy, too."

"So, prove it. Watch him for me."

Onnie sighed. "Alright, Clarissa. But you'd better call him this time."

"I'll call. I just got busy last time. You know I love my boy, Onnie."

"I know you do."

Clarissa spoke softer. "Just make sure he don't go nowhere near that Shiloh or his granddaddy, you hear? It's off limits."

"You know I won't let him go there, Clarissa. You should know better than anybody."

"There's a white girl staring through the screen!" The boy yelled.

All eyes bounced to the door where I stood. I stumbled backwards on the porch.

"Onnie, who's that?"

"Come on in, child, and meet my family."

I didn't want to meet that lady. She squinted her eyes and crossed her arms. The boy on the sofa just stared. I opened the door. Its screech echoed through the silent awkwardness.

"Tara, this is my daughter Clarissa."

"Stepdaughter." The lady said.

Onnie ignored her. "And this is her boy Darren. He's eleven."

Darren didn't say anything. I didn't know what to say. I wanted to tell these people to get out of Onnie's house. I wanted to tell them to leave us alone. "It's nice to meet you." I said instead.

Clarissa looked me over, then turned to Onnie. "What do you think you're doing, letting this white girl in your house? Are you crazy? Them white folks ain't going to like that one bit."

"You let me worry about that." She waved a dismissive hand at me. "Tara, why don't you take Darren outside and play. Go on down to the railroad tracks and play on the empty cars. Darren will like that."

"Does she know about Shiloh?" Clarissa asked.

"She knows. Don't you worry. Tara will stay clear away from there. Now kids, go on outside now."

Darren shrugged and walked over to switch off the television set.

I had never played with a black boy before. He didn't seem to know what to do, either.

Outside he decided to speak to me. "You can just go, you know. I don't play with girls. I especially don't play with no white girls."

"Onnie wants me to play with you."

"She just wanted me out of the house so she could talk to my mama. She don't fool nobody." He kicked an empty coke bottle down the road as we walked. Once we reached it, he kicked it again. The hollow sound of his foot against the glass preceded the scrape of the bottle against the hard dirt.

"So, you're staying here with Onnie?" I already knew the answer and didn't like it. I stuck my foot out and kicked the bottle before he could.

He stopped and switched his direction toward Onnie's house again. "I guess."

"Don't you want to?"

"Not really, but mamas do what mamas do."

That one I understood. I felt guilty for wanting him gone.

"Well, well. Look who's back today." A voice said behind us.

It was those boys from the first day I met Onnie.

"And she has a new friend." The shorter one said.

"What are you hanging out here with black folks for? Don't you have any white friends?" Another boy asked.

"I'm not bothering you." I said.

"Hey, it's cool." Tyrone said. "If Onnie likes you, you must be okay. Where ya headed?"

I wasn't sure if I should trust him. My cousins said black boys are natural born criminals. But then I decided to echo his words in my head. If Onnie liked him, he must be okay.

"We're just going down to the tracks to play on the empty train cars."

"Who's your friend?"

"Darren. He's Onnie's grandson."

"Yeah, I've seen you before. Been a while, though." Tyrone reached out to Darren, and they did that funny handshake thing that I had seen on TV. It ended with Tyrone's fist on top of Darren's.

"We've got something better to do. You in for some fun?"

"Tyrone, I don't think that's a good idea." A chubby boy with a rock band on his t-shirt spoke up.

"C'mon, man. This kid's little. He can sneak in and out and no one would notice him." He turned back to Darren. "How'd you like to make ten bucks?"

Ten dollars sounded nice. I rarely had any money of my own. "What do you want us to do?"

"Not you. You'd stick out like a marshmallow with that fair skin." The other boys laughed.

Darren, who had been quiet, spoke up. "We ain't stealin' for you. I don't want to go to Juvy."

The boys laughed aloud, slapping each other. "How does a punk kid like you know about Juvy?" Tyrone asked.

"I just know. And I ain't going there."

"Naw, boy, it ain't nothing like that. You see, I got a girl. She lives in that shack town Shiloh. Her daddy is as mean as— well, let's just say he's mean. I need you to take this note to her and bring back one from her to me." He pulled out a note that was folded into one of those paper stars. I had always wanted to learn how to fold my paper like that.

"I can't go back to Shiloh." I shook my head vehemently.

"Back there? You been there before?"

"Yes, and Onnie had to help me. A man grabbed me."

"I'm not surprised. You being a white girl. Blonde, too." There was a time when I wouldn't have known what he meant. Thanks to the Candy Man, I knew. "But again, you ain't being asked."

He looked back at Darren. "What about you, man? I'll give you the whole ten dollars."

Darren shrugged and said, "Why can't one of them go?" He nodded his head at the other boys.

Tyrone shook his head. "It can't be anyone that her daddy's seen before. You're just a kid. He won't notice a kid."

"How will I find her?"

"I'll show you the house from the woods."

Darren put his hands in his pockets. "Alright, but when will I get the ten bucks?"

"When you come back."

He shook his head. "Nope. I want five before and five after." I both admired and envied Darren's boldness.

"Okay, but if you don't follow through, I'll take those five bucks back. Deal?"

Darren reached out and shook his hand. Tyrone pulled out five dollars from his pocket and handed it to Darren. He shoved in down into his sock.

"You're not going to Shiloh, Darren. I'll tell Onnie. Give him back the money." I said.

"No way. Ten bucks for delivering a couple of notes. I'm going. And if you don't tell, I'll give you two dollars."

Tyrone stepped up to me. He looked down and crossed his arms. "She won't tell. If she does, I'll go tell her mama that she spends so much time over here in Color Town."

I sighed. He had me. That's the last thing I wanted. Tyrone reminded me of Albert. If someone stood in his way of getting what he wanted, he bullied them into moving out of the way.

I decided to follow them. If Darren got into trouble, maybe I could help, or get Onnie in time.

The boys paid no attention to me. They stood at the edge of the woods near the clearing on the right side of Shiloh creek facing the tracks.

A mosquito landed on my arm as I stood behind them. I slapped it away.

"See it? It has that clothesline with all the baby clothes on it. She has a little sister. Anyway, go to that window in the back right behind that big sheet on the line. Tap on her window and hand her the note when she opens the window. Her name is Shay. As soon as you tell her the note is from me, you hand it off, wait for one from her, and run back here. Don't wait. Got it?"

"Got it." Darren looked like he was losing his nerve already. "What if her daddy catches me?"

"Don't let him."

"But what if he does?"

"Then you won't see these five bucks." He held up the bill. I think Darren knew he'd have more to worry about than the five dollars at that point, but now his male ego motivated him as much as the money.

He bent down to tie his shoe. "Okay, I'm ready."

Tyrone handed him the note and they exchanged the hand-shake again. My stomach flipped when he began walking down the sloped grass filled with bee clover. The mosquito returned and circled around my head with its low buzz. I followed it with my eyes and snapped the tiny nuisance within my palmed fist. I squished hard, then opened my fist to see its bloody remains flattened against my skin. Wiping it on my shorts, I looked back to Shiloh. Darren had already made it to the clothesline but stood still behind a sheet. A man paced in front of the house smoking a cigarette. He was a good head taller than the line. He had on suspenders which held his pants up over his bulging belly. Tyrone cursed under his breath. He sounded like my pa-paw when he slammed the hammer down onto his thumb. The man put out his cigarette and walked away from the clothesline. He walked back into the house. Darren stepped out from behind the sheet and crept up to the window with the pink curtain. We could see him tapping softly on the pane. It seemed like an hour had passed. Finally, a girl about Tyrone's age appeared. She frowned until Darren held up the note. She smiled, looked behind her, and then opened the window. She said something to Darren, took the note, then held up her hand for Darren to wait. She returned with another note and gave it to Darren before closing the window and curtain. I sighed relief. It was over. Darren would have his money and I didn't have to go back to tell Onnie and that snotty woman their boy was in trouble.

"Looks like your buddy pulled it off." Tyrone said to me. Darren stopped to tie his shoe again. He didn't notice that the man had come back outside.

"Hey, boy! What are you doing in my yard?"

Darren jumped up and took off like a shot. He was a fast runner, but not fast enough. The man caught up to him in a few strides. "Are you stealing from me?" The man had his thick arms around Darren who kicked and hollered for him to let go.

"I ain't letting you go 'til you get a whoopin' boy. I know you don't live around here so either you was stealing from me or going to. Let me see your pockets!"

"I ain't stealin' nothin' from you. Let me go!"

That man reached down into Darren's blue jeans pocket and pulled out that girl's note. His face turned redder than Papaw's tractor. "You seeing my girl? Naw. You too young. Whose note is this? Is this for that lowlife hoodlum Tyrone? Where is he?" The man scanned the area in our direction.

Tyrone didn't wait. He took off running and left me to witness what happened to Darren.

"You tell me whose note this is, boy."

"I don't have to tell you nothin'!"

"You tell me now or you'll get the whoopin' you askin' for, sneakin' around my house like the little vagrant you are."

"I ain't no vagrant."

"How would you know? You probably don't know what a vagrant is! I'll tell you what it is. It's someone like that Tyrone, that's what it is. And if you hangin' around him, you is a vagrant, too. Now tell me, whose note is this?"

Darren just stared at him.

The man held Darren with one hand and took his belt off with the other. Darren's eyes grew large, and he started squirming to get out of the man's grasp. The man was too strong, though, and he drug Darren to a nearby rusty barrel. He forced Darren down onto the barrel and started swinging that leather belt down onto Darren's bottom. I couldn't take it. I started running toward them, screaming at the man to stop. Surprised, the man stopped to see what made such a noise. Darren kicked him in the shin and started running.

"C'mon!" He grabbed me by the arm, and we started running back to the woods. We didn't look back to see if he was following. We just ran and ran until we reached the street that ran in front of Onnie's house.

Tyrone stood with the other boys and laughed at us as we panted and walked toward them.

"You owe me five bucks." Darren said.

"Oh, no I don't. You didn't deliver the other note, the one meant for me. So you owe me five bucks. Give it back." He held out his hand. The other boys flanked his sides, intimidating us with their menacing stares.

"But he did deliver your note to her." I said.

"That wasn't the deal. The whole job had to be done or else he forfeited the ten bucks. Now hand it over."

Darren sighed and gave back the five bucks. Tyrone snatched it and shook his head as he placed it back in his pocket. "I might have known a little coward like you couldn't get it done."

I wanted to shout that he was the one who was hiding in the trees while Darren braved his mission. I wanted to shout that he and his buddies were the cowards, but I had shouted enough for one afternoon.

# 8

"There's alligators in that river." Albert said this one afternoon when we were picking the muscadine grapes for Mamaw's jelly. Mamaw cooked or made things often in those days. She had a primitive kitchen with minimal conveniences, but she managed to make jams and jellies, canned fruits and vegetables, and baked breads and pies that would have put any store-bought items to shame. I liked picking muscadines because they were tastiest right off the vine.

Albert spat a muscadine seed at me. He laughed.

"There ain't no alligators in there. You're just trying to scare me. Mamaw wouldn't let us on this riverbank if there were."

"She's the one that told me about them. Ask her." He threw up a grape and caught it with his mouth.

The Yazoo River looked more like a swamp than a river with its green slime coating the top of the water. Rotten logs stretched from the bank onto the slimed surface. Some had broken away from their bank roots and floated to the other side, rocking, and bobbing with the slow current of the river.

"I bet an alligator as big as that log could be on this bank in seconds. Then you would be gator food." He popped another grape into his mouth and crunched down for emphasis.

"If that's true, then why aren't you scared?"

"I'm a fast runner and you're not."

It wasn't true. I was really fast. I had won relays with blue ribbons at school. But Albert was faster. He beat me at everything and always bragged about it. Just once I'd like to beat him at something. Mama said once that I needed to feel sorry for him because his mama ran off and left him. It was hard to feel sorry for him when he was so mean.

Sometimes Albert was fun to play with. He came up with some great ideas. Like the time we set up a two by four on top of one of Pawpaw's old barrels and made a seesaw. Or when we used that same old barrel to roll each other around the yard. The headache I got from all that jostling was worth the thrill. He even saved me from a snake bite once. I was only six and that snake was inches from my hand as we climbed a tree from Pawpaw's orchard to reach some pears at the top. Albert snatched that snake right up and flung it across the cotton field beyond the orchard. Sometimes I forced myself to remember the snake-slinging Albert when he was doing things like spitting muscadine seeds at me or scaring me with alligator talk.

No one really spoke about Albert's mama. Uncle Brody married her several years before the war. I had read in school about how they didn't even call it a war, but Mamaw did. She said a young man ought not to see the things those boys saw and have to do the things those boys did in that war. I had heard her tell her friend Irene that Uncle Brody had to shoot a young boy in order to save his whole unit from an explosive strapped to the boy's body. She didn't know I was listening, but I couldn't look at my uncle without thinking about that.

"My Brody was a church goin' young man, never smoked or drank or cussed. That war took my sweet boy and sent back a stranger." Mamaw had told Irene.

Uncle Brody definitely smoked and drank and cussed now. He was the reason I knew words I shouldn't know. When he drank, his booming, loud voice hollered more than it spoke. Albert and Sam were scared of him, even though he was their daddy. Uncle Brody's head almost hit the ceiling and he had to bend down to walk through doorways. Still, I liked him. When I climbed into his long lap, he'd say, "Whatcha climbing on me for?" Then, he'd pat me and let me stay while he watched T.V. We never talked, just sat together. He liked to eat pretzels while he watched T.V. Every few minutes, he'd hand me the bag and let me share. Since that night with the Candy Man, I hadn't sat on Uncle Brody's lap again.

"You're eating more muscadines than you're putting in the bucket." I said to Albert.

"Mind your own business." Albert shoved me and I lost my footing. I started to slide down the riverbank. Panic from alligator talk, and also drowning since I couldn't swim, forced me to drop my bucket of muscadines and grab onto a root vine sticking out of the ground. My left foot went into the water. I shut my eyes and kicked and hollered. The more I tried to pull myself up, the more the root came out of the ground, dropping like a rope and lowering me down into the river.

Remembering the snake-slinging Albert, I yelled, "Albert, help me!"

Albert didn't move. He stared past me with eyes the size of Mamaw's biscuits. I looked over my shoulder and watched as it moved toward me. The alligator had large eyes and a large mouth. Its bumpy back stuck out of the water. It wasn't in a hurry, but I was. This time, I screamed so loud my throat hurt, but I didn't care. I just couldn't get eaten by an alligator. There was no worse way to die.

Hands grabbed onto my arms and pulled me up. Uncle Brody planted my feet onto the top of the riverbank and swatted my bottom good. I was crying too hard to ask him why.

"What fool reason could you have for scaring a man to death? I thought you'd been hurt."

"The alligator..." I looked down at the river. The alligator had stopped against the bank. "It's right there!" I grabbed Uncle Brody's arm and pointed.

Laughter erupted from Uncle Brody's chest. I had never heard him laugh before, and had I not been terrified out of my mind, I would have probably stopped to appreciate it, but this stunned me, so I just stared at him.

"Baby girl, that's no alligator. You were screaming over a tree stump."

I looked back at the river, but I didn't see a tree stump. I saw a monster wanting to eat me. I shook my head.

"C'mon." He picked me up and walked sideways down the bank.

"No!" I started squirming out of his arms.

"Hush! I'm going to show you what you're so afraid of."

If Uncle Brody was right, then I knew I'd look foolish, but if he was wrong, it wouldn't matter if he looked foolish because we'd be eaten to death.

Uncle Brody stuck his foot on that alligator and pushed. Sure enough, it went backward. Then, it turned over and bobbed up and down. That's when it looked like a stump. A stump that had knots for eyes, and a split on the end for its mouth. An alligator stump.

Mortified, I wiped my tears while Uncle Brody laughed and carried me back up the bank. We picked up all the muscadines and walked back to the house. Mamaw waited on the porch with Albert who didn't have his usual smirk expression. Even when Uncle Brody told the story inside the house and everybody laughed, Albert didn't laugh. I think he, like me, had been so sure that he had seen an alligator.

Once I heard a saying, "Fear becomes its object when we invite it to". I now know that's exactly what Albert and I did on the Yazoo River. I never told on Albert for scaring me with alligator talk. He never thanked me or even mentioned it, but something changed in him after that day. He didn't bully me anymore. When I told Onnie about it, she said, "Sometimes when we're faced with the fear of losing something, it don't matter how much we didn't value it up 'til then. All of a sudden, we hold on to it a bit tighter and treat it better than before. Sometimes our greatest treasures are discovered after we lose them."

I didn't know if Albert treasured me or not, but I knew I shouldn't have to almost lose my legs to an alligator log to find out how much I treasure them.

# 9

I learned how to disappear when Mama had the reverend over. She pretended I didn't know, and I pretended she was right. He made his visits to our house on Wednesdays and Saturdays. That's when I'd visit Onnie and Darren. He had been here a couple weeks now and since that day at Shiloh, we got along just fine. One particular hot day, Onnie sat on the porch with us while we ate orange push-ups that Onnie had brought us from the store. Darren pushed his last piece out of the paper, but just as he opened his mouth for the creamy bite, it dropped onto the porch. I giggled and he shrugged.

"I was full anyway." he said.

"If you were full, why would you take another bite?" Onnie said. She laughed as she fanned herself with a folded newspaper. "That's what's wrong with you young'uns. Old'uns, too, I reckon. Always taking more than they really need or want. Seems to me like we'd all be better off like the Good Lord says."

"What does He say?" I asked.

"To be content."

"What's content?" Darren asked this time.

"It's when you understand that you already have it pretty good and don't have to ask for no more, but if God decides to bless you with more, you'll thank Him, take a little, and share a lot."

I looked at my push-up in my hand and handed it to Darren. He smiled at me and took it. We didn't worry as much about germs in those days, so we enjoyed ourselves more.

"Onnie", he asked, "Why are you always thinking about God?"

She sighed and stopped rocking. "I guess 'cause He's always thinking about me."

"Is He always thinking about me?" Darren asked.

"Why yes, He is, boy. Yes, He is. He thinks about Tara, too." She winked at me, but I didn't say anything. It didn't feel polite to argue after eating the treat she bought me.

"Did my mama live here with you when she was young?" Darren asked.

Onnie sat back and closed her eyes. She started humming that church song she always sang.

Darren and I knew that meant she wasn't going to answer. We decided to play cards. We were still playing when a man and woman asked to see Onnie. I had seen them before. They lived in Color Town just a row of houses over. We told them she was inside, so they knocked. Moments later, Onnie gave us a dollar each and told us to go to the corner store and buy us another push-up or a coke. In those days, cokes meant any soda. When we got to the store, the man gave us a pack of peanuts to put in our cokes. I had seen Uncle Brody do this, but never tried it myself. Excited, we poured them in and felt like we had hit the treat jackpot that day.

When we came back, we heard angry voices inside the house.

"You listen here, Onnie! We don't want no trouble. Now I know you is a god-fearing woman, and you want to be kind to that white girl, but-"

"Her name is Tara, Fred. The Good Lord calls her by her name. So should we."

He swore under his breath. "Look around you, Onnie. Do you think we're called by name same as she is? Why you stuck in this Hell hole you're in?"

"I'll ask you to mind your tongue, Fredrick Sanders, or you'll leave my house."

"She doesn't belong here, Onnie."

"Don't you see you doin' to her what they do to us? She needs me, Fred. And I need her."

"We need you, too, Onnie." This time the woman spoke. "We don't want no trouble around here and little white girls hanging around a color neighborhood can't be no good for nobody."

"It's good for her, and it's good for me. Darren has taken to her, too."

"It's not about her personally, Onnie. It's about black and white. It's about white folks not wanting us to have anything to do with their children. There'll be trouble. You mark my words." He slapped his hand down onto her kitchen table.

Darren whispered to me, "I've seen them at church with Onnie."

I nodded. It didn't feel nice being talked about like that. Of all places, I thought I belonged at Onnie's house more than anywhere. Now these people were saying I didn't.

"I'd better go." I whispered to Darren. He frowned. I set my soda down on the steps and ran all the way home. The reverend's car was parked out back, hidden from the road like it always was on Wednesdays. I decided to keep walking. I had to try to see Cindy every Wednesday now anyway to cover my tracks with Mama, so I figured I'd just go early. I pulled the end of my shirt up to my eyes to wipe them dry. I didn't want Cindy to see I had been crying. She had been asking too many questions lately about the bruises on my face, arms, and legs.

Cindy and I ran up and down the cotton rows, our bare feet slapping the dry dirt.

I showed her how to pick the bolls without leaving strands of seeded fluff behind.

"Are we supposed to do this?" she asked.

"We're not taking enough to put a dent in it anyway. Look!" I pointed to the other side of the field.

"What?" She shaded her eyes with her hand to block out the midday sun that obscured her view.

"It's a cotton trailer! C'mon!" I grabbed her hand and raced toward the big, red, metal container. I looked all around us. Papaw had told me not to climb into a cotton trailer full of cotton because I could ruin the fresh bolls, but I had always imagined how fun it would be to bounce around on top of the pile. I thought it would be like walking on clouds. I almost voiced my thoughts to Cindy but thought better of it.

I started climbing. Cindy followed. I swung my leg over and my foot hit the softness. We were bouncing and giggling in minutes. We rolled and jumped until we tired out, then we lied on our backs and talked.

"Isn't it funny how we're lying on clouds, looking up at clouds?" I asked her.

"You're so weird, Tara."

I sat up. "Maybe we should get out of here before someone see us." I climbed down, the joy of moments before had already disappeared with Cindy's words. She couldn't have known that my mama had often said that very thing over and over. Still, it stung.

She chattered as we walked back through the cotton toward the river. She didn't seem to notice how quiet I'd become. I was often quiet in those days, so no one noticed when I was quieter.

"What's that colored boy doing here?" I looked where she pointed and there stood Darren, watching us from the trees that lined the river.

I said nothing as we approached him.

"You'd better get out of here. This is her papaw's land. He'll shoot you if he catches you on his land."

Darren looked at me. "Is that true?"

"No. He won't shoot you, but you'd better go."

He stared at me for what seemed an eternity, then he turned around and walked away.

"Who does he think he is? They're getting bolder and bolder. My daddy said pretty soon they'll take over the whole country."

"I'd better go home now, Cindy. It's getting late." We said our goodbyes, so I ran to catch up to Darren.

"Darren, wait!"

He stopped.

"I'm sorry about that. Cindy doesn't mean it."

"Yes, she does."

"Well, anyway, we can go back and play now if you want to. Cindy and I bounced on the cotton in that trailer over there. It's fun. C'mon, I'll show you."

"No, thanks. Onnie wanted me to bring you back, but I can see you're okay. Go on back to your white friend."

"I can't go back to Onnie's house, Darren. You heard those people. I'll bring trouble to Onnie."

"She said for you not to pay them no mind. She said to come get you, but you no worse than those people in Onnie's house. They made you feel unwelcome at Onnie's, but you just made me feel unwelcome, too. I guess those folks be right. Blacks and whites can't mix." He walked away toward Color Town. I turned back to go to my house, but I only took a few steps before sitting down in the middle of the road.

"Why were you talking to that black boy?"

Cindy. She had come back. Did she hear about Onnie?

"Do you know him?"

"No." Shame filled my face with heat.

"I saw you, Tara. I heard you, too. You know that boy."

"So what? I've seen him around a time or two. It's no law against talking to him, is it?"

"My daddy says if we play with black boys, we'll marry black boys."

I didn't care what her daddy said. I didn't care about who I'd marry since I'd already decided I wouldn't. I just wanted to be Darren's friend again.

"Well, I'm not playing with him. I was just talking to him."

"If you want to be my friend, you can't talk to black people."

"But why? If they're nice, why can't I talk to them?"

"You just can't."

"That's not a reason."

"Make up your mind, Tara. It's him or me." She didn't look like the friend I liked anymore. She looked just like my mama when I had displeased her. Same tone, same eyes.

"Fine. I choose him." I ran to catch up to Darren.

—ele—

Sunday at church, Cindy sat with another girl a bit younger than us. She gave her candy and they passed notes. Occasionally, they'd glance over at me and whisper and giggle. I sat alone by my mama. She and the reverend spoke to each other as if they only saw each other at church. He called her "Ms. Ellie", and she called him "Reverend Martin".

He preached on God's love and how the Lord never plays favorites. I looked over at Cindy and her new best friend. Two rows back, Mrs. Martin sat stoically in her seat, her eyes staring blankly at her husband. I still held the tootsie roll The Candy Man had pressed into my palm earlier. I looked back at him. He winked. Mama reached around the pew and subtly pinched my arm to make me turn around. I jumped and she pinched harder. I stilled.

I didn't care what Reverend Martin said. God did play favorites. And I wasn't one of them.

---

That week Mama took me on what she called a "Mom and me" day. We went to the Coca Cola plant in Greenwood and watched how they bottled the drinks. Then, she took me to Pizza Inn buffet, and we had our favorite pizza, taco pizza. I ate until my stomach stretched against my jeans. She told me how pretty I was turning out to be and thanked me for being such a good girl because she's had such a hard time being a single mother.

"I have a surprise for you."

"You do?"

"Yes. Would you like to have a new father?"

"A new what?"

"Father. I think it's about time, don't you?"

I didn't know what to say to that, so I didn't say anything.

"Anyway, we'll talk about it later. Some things have to be worked out first."

I didn't want to think about what things, or who she'd be working them out with.

# 10

"**C**an those people make me stay away from you, Onnie?" I asked her this as we worked on a 400-piece puzzle one afternoon. I spoke up so she could hear me over the box fan plugged into an extension cord running from the house underneath the screen door. Darren stopped trying to force an inside piece where it didn't belong and waited with me for her answer.

"I suppose they could if they wanted to." She wiped a trickle of sweat from her hairline with her apron. Onnie had the longest fingers. I had heard once that people with long fingers could play the piano well. If that were true, Onnie would be excellent at it. Mrs. Martin played the piano. She had long fingers, too. I had always wanted to play, but my mama couldn't afford lessons. I didn't have any talents. I couldn't even put a puzzle together. I sighed.

"Onnie, is it just white folks who are racists?"

Darren spoke up. "Of course, it is. White folks always be hatin' on black folks." I didn't like his nasty voice. It didn't sound like Darren.

Onnie shook her head. "Now there you go."

"What?" Darren asked.

"There you go, answering her question, but not with the answer you intended."

We both scrunched our faces.

"What does that mean, Onnie?" I asked.

"Darren just showed you how black folks have their own ideas about white folks; just as white folks have their ideas about black folks. Problem is, neither side really thinks about God's idea about all of us."

Darren rolled his eyes. "Now there you go, Onnie."

"What?"

"You know, saying all folks is the same and all that. Just jive talkin' to me. We ain't the same, Onnie. And that's the problem. We won't ever be the same."

"No, you won't. Ain't supposed to be. At least not all the way. What's the same is how we act as human beings. Take your answer just now. Does Tara hate you?"

He frowned. "No."

"There ya go. She's white. You said 'white folks always be hatin' on black folks."

"But she's just one white girl. The others hate us."

"What others? You have had how many encounters in your eleven years?"

I felt somehow vindicated, but then Onnie turned to me.

"And what about you? You think 'cause you willing to come over here and talk and laugh and play with Darren that you don't have the wrong ideas about us?"

I didn't know what to say.

"Don't get me wrong, I think you're learning and you're teaching us, too. We can learn from one another about the ways we're different, and the ways we're alike."

"Just look at this puzzle. So many pieces, so many colors. But at the end of the day, they all have the same purpose. To make a complete picture. It's the same with mankind. God made us different shapes and sizes, and all kinds of colors, but ultimately, we're here for His design. His purpose. And He wants all of us to fit together in that design." She stood up. "Now, you kids go play and think on that while you're at it. I'm going inside to put on some supper."

"Makes sense what she said." I told Darren.

"I guess. Anyhow, it don't matter none. Can't force a puzzle piece where it don't want to go."

_ele_

"David's moving back in with us." Mama shocked me with those words that afternoon. I found her in the kitchen, making his favorite, fried chicken. She stuck her fingers into the Crisco oil can and scooped out a glop of thick, white goo, dropping it into the black iron skillet. My mama loved her iron skillets. She had two, and I learned at about the same number of years the importance of cleaning those skillets properly. When she took the skillets out of the cabinets, it was always a good day.

"Why?" I asked.

"What do you mean, why? We're still married, so he's moving back in."

David had been my stepfather for all of two months before he left. I wanted to ask her if this was the new father she talked about. I wanted to ask what about the preacher, but I didn't dare.

"Where is he?"

"He's loading up his things from the trailer park in town. He'll be here for dinner. I want you to set the table and make him feel welcome. How about you help me make cornbread? Get the other skillet out and ready." She smiled and bent down to kiss my cheek. She grabbed the yellow Tupperware canister off the countertop and passed it to me. I knew what to do so I measured out the amount of cornmeal into the glass bowl. Adding the other ingredients, I stirred while Mama chatted with me. She hadn't talked to me this much in weeks. As she reached her arms around me and helped me to stir the cornmeal, I thought about Darren's mom. Onnie was right. We were all just pieces in a puzzle. And sometimes the pieces just didn't want to fit. But when they did, it was a beautiful picture.

I got used to David being in the house again. He didn't talk to me much, but at least he and Mama got along. I could hear them in the bedroom at night. I didn't like it, but it made Mama happy for him to be there, and at least the preacher didn't come around anymore. At least they weren't hurting Mrs. Martin. At least she wasn't hitting me.

David drank beer. Lots of it, but he only drank at night on the weekends. When he did, he acted silly. One night, he jumped up and grabbed me, picked me up and danced all around the living room. I giggled, and he ducked me down, but my head hit the floor with a thud, then he lost his balance and fell backwards.

He got up, then walked back to his chair. "Some dance partner you are, little bit." He laughed and opened another beer. I rubbed the back of my head and went back to my room. Nothing had really changed with David and me. I didn't really know him anymore now than when he had lived here before. New father? I didn't think so. I wanted to be happy he was back. After all, my mama acted so much better with him in the house. But she also spent less time with me and more on him. At least without him, we'd sometimes have fun days where we cooked, or played outside, or went shopping. Now, she spent her hours off work with him. They'd leave me at home and go riding off to who knows where. Then, when they got home, they'd often disappear into the bedroom. The best nights were when we'd watch the Sunday night movies on television. Mama would make popcorn and we three would sit and watch together. David would bring home sweets and sodas, too, and hand them to me, saying, "Here's a treat, Tara Gail. It's movie night."

We didn't go to church anymore. David didn't like it. I was glad I didn't have to see Reverend Martin or Cindy and her new best friend anymore, and especially the Candy Man. That was the best part of David moving back.

Papaw didn't like David. He never said so, but I could tell. Mamaw didn't say much, either.

---

Late July we all got together for a picnic at Grenada Lake. This was a family event and my cousins, and I looked forward to it every year. Mamaw always brought along the ice cream maker, and we kids had to take turns cranking the handle. The ice cream took so long to make. We turned and turned, then Mamaw poured the rock salt in, and we turned some more. To my delight, I could sneak a piece of that rock salt and pop it into my mouth before anyone saw me. Mamaw didn't want us eating that salt. She said it was bad for us and we'd end up like her brother, my great uncle Harold, who had died with high blood pressure. Somehow, I just couldn't equate eating a piece of rock salt every year at our summer picnic to my Uncle Harold's health, but I never said anything to argue. No one argued with Mamaw Webb unless you wanted an hour-long lecture to ruin your appetite. One thing I could say about Mamaw Webb, though. She sure knew how to put the fixings on a picnic. There were watermelons, fried chicken, potato salad, macaroni and cheese, chips and dips, sodas and lemonade, and sandwiches. There were pies to go with the ice cream, and what Papaw always called the best banana pudding a man could put in his pie hole. I thought it was weird that he'd say that when it wasn't pie he was eating.

I couldn't help but think about Darren and Onnie. They'd like this picnic. If we were all being the puzzle pieces we should be, we'd all fit in. I could invite them along to make a mighty fine picture.

"What are they doing here?" Albert pointed down the beach at black people doing the same thing we were. We all looked, and my uncle swore. "What'd I tell you? You let one family in, then the rest of 'em start pouring in."

"As long as they stay on their side of the lake, and we stay on ours, what do you care?" Mamaw said. "They got a right to be here same as you."

I didn't want to stay around and listen anymore. I walked down to the beach and dipped my toes in the water.

"Tara Gail!" Mama shouted at me from the picnic table. "No swimming until that food settles, you hear me?"

"Yes ma'am." I sat down and wiggled my toes in the wet sand. A dragonfly landed on my foot, but I didn't scare it away. I liked dragonflies. Laughter floated from down the beach. I saw the black family, laughing aloud and talking just like my family did every year. Funny, I never noticed how they acted the same. I decided to take a walk and asked Albert and Sam to go with me.

"Ya'll stay away from the lake now, and don't go too far." Mamaw said.

"Hey, look at those paddle boats!" Sam said. "Do you think Daddy will let us ride today?"

"He's in a pretty good mood, so maybe." Albert said. "Let's go see the graveyard."

To get to the little graveyard nearby, we had to cross a little bridge. Sam didn't like it. He had an unhealthy fear of bridges. He held on to my arm so tight, I thought he'd bore a hole into it.

We finally came to the little fenced-in graveyard with the peculiar statues and names. Albert had a fascination with ghost stories, so he started telling one and scaring us. The grave-yard was spooky. Although we could hear the distant activity from the beach, the graveyard, with its surrounding woods and stillness, proved eerie when set against the ominous nature of Albert's ghostly voice.

"Boo!" he screamed at just the right time. I expected it, so I didn't jump.

"Stop it, Albert!" Sam yelled. He picked up a stick and threw it at his brother. Albert laughed and started chasing him. They left me behind at the graveyard. I didn't want to run. The heat made me ready to go back to swim, so I started walking toward the bridge.

"Wait up!" I yelled, but I could hear their voices far ahead.

I walked a ways but realized that wasn't my cousins' voices shouting. When I reached the bridge, I saw a black man and a little boy about four years old on the other side of the bridge. I ducked behind a tree.

"I told you not to run off! Didn't I tell you?"

The little boy nodded with his head down.

The man reached out and struck the boy across the face. I flinched. The boy dropped to his knees, holding his cheek, sob-bing. The man reached down and pulled his belt from his pants. I couldn't watch. I ran back to the graveyard and sat down at a baby's grave. I hugged the little concrete cherub and cried for that little black boy whose name I didn't even know. One thing

I did know, though. Onnie was right. Blacks and whites were much more alike than we all realized.

# 11

M y aunt showed up at the picnic. Well, she wasn't really my aunt anymore. I heard Mama and Mamaw talking about how Uncle Brody had finally signed the divorce papers.

Aunt Diane didn't show up alone. Her new husband Jesse had his arm around her as they strolled up to the picnic area. Aunt Diane wore a green bikini with lemons all over it. he had on one of those swimsuits that looked like underwear. They were red with white drawstrings, and his belly flopped down over them, almost hiding the strings. Mamaw mumbled something about the thick rug on his chest. She didn't like hairy men. I didn't, either. My papaw and Uncle Brody didn't have hair on their chest, so I guess I just figured men weren't supposed to have it.

Albert and Sam hugged their mama, but I could tell they weren't too fond of the hairy stranger rubbing the tops of their heads. They begged Mamaw to let us go swimming.

"Aren't you going to stay here with your mama for a bit? I haven't seen you in months."

"Whose fault is that?" Uncle Brody grumbled from his reclining beach chair. He popped the beer can open and swallowed a huge gulp.

Everyone pretended not to hear him.

I followed the boys down to the sandy shore. The sand burned the arches of my feet, so I wasted no time wading out in the lake until it surrounded my waist with its cold, murky water.

Sometimes the lake scared me. Last year a man had been killed when he swam into a bed of water moccasins. He had yelled out, "Barbed wire!" Uncle Brody said it must've been a terror filled moment when he realized that barbed wire wasn't barbed wire. Mamaw hushed him when she realized I had listened. She told me that man had been skiing and that those snakes were close to the bushy shore, and that we didn't have to worry about snakes off the little beached area where we swam. Still, I couldn't help looking around nervously. The idea that something could get my legs before I could even know it swam there terrified me.

"You know there's sharks in this lake?"

"No, there's not. It's not the ocean." Sam argued.

"But it feeds from the ocean so sometimes sharks swim in here."

"Shut up, Albert. Sam, there's no sharks. The lake has land all around it so the ocean can't get through." Although Albert didn't bully me as much, he certainly didn't let up on his brother.

"See? I knew it." Sam splashed water at Albert, and they began their usual horseplay. I didn't like horseplay in the water, so I swam away a bit to avoid getting pushed under. That's when I felt it. Something brushed my leg. It wasn't lake debris, either. I kicked my legs and hit something. Screaming, I start swimming toward the beach. I could see everyone at the picnic area, and they weren't looking my way. Albert and Sam had gone back to get the floating rings.

A head surfaced right in front of me. It was Aunt Diane's new hairy husband.

"Did I scare you?" He laughed. He picked me up and tossed me away from him. I splashed with force and went under the water. Then, his hands grabbed me again under the water on my stomach and behind my neck to throw me again. I screamed and kicked, surprising him. He let go of me and swam away.

Mamaw yelled, "Tara, come crank the Ice Cream maker!" Albert and Sam ran past me, carrying their floating rings and I wondered why they didn't have to help make ice cream. Still, I'd rather have cranked ice cream than be in that water with him.

Jesse watched me as he tread water. I made my way to shore in seconds.

"Tara, you're shivering. Put this towel on you." Mama wrapped me in the towel and David pulled me close and dried my hair with another beach towel.

"Let her crank the ice cream in the sun, Mama." Uncle Brody said. His eyes were on Aunt Diane who busied herself with the camera. She attached the long flash bulb to the top of the camera, then walked down to get a picture of Jesse wrestling with the boys in the water.

"Did you invite her here?" Uncle Brody asked Mamaw.

"Now, why you'd go and ask that for?" Papaw asked. "You know better than that."

Uncle Brody stood up and threw his beer can into the nearby garbage bin. "I don't know why she came."

Mamaw sighed. "They're her boys. She should see them."

"Her boys? She left them over a year ago. I provide for them; you help me tend to them. What right does she have to 'em?"

I didn't think she had much of a right, either, but I wasn't old enough to have my opinion valued so I focused on the ice cream. Screams from the water made our heads turn. Jesse had both boys on his shoulders, then fell backwards into the water. The boys begged to do it again. Uncle Brody opened another beer can.

"I wish you wouldn't drink that stuff around the kids," Mamaw said.

"I don't have to be here. You're the one who insisted I come along today. Had I known she'd show up, I would've stayed home and drank my beer in peace." He got up and walked off down the trail his boys and I took just an hour earlier.

"Leave him be, Mama." My mama said. "He's had it hard with the Vietnam war."

"Can only blame a war for so long, Ellie. Then, it's an excuse, not a cause." Papaw said.

Papaw knew about war. He had been in World War II and fought the Nazis. Unlike my uncle, he regaled us with stories about his time overseas. Once, when he was eating in the mess hall tent, a bomb raid hit his camp. Well, Papaw didn't want to give up his only good meal of the day, so he said he jumped up, grabbed his plate, and hit the fox hole, shoving his food into his mouth as men scrambled in beside him. He said he'd just as soon die with a full stomach than an empty one.

My papaw liked to eat, but he wasn't a big man. In fact, no one in our family had any weight issues. Mamaw's waist looked like a pencil next to many women her age. Yet here we were on a picnic, with pies, cakes, and ice cream. Papaw said Mamaw could eat the Yazoo River and you wouldn't know it to look at her. Mamaw said she worked too hard to get fat.

She never stopped doing things. I watched as she shook the ice cream canister into the bowl she had packed and then proceeded to dish it out equally into little Styrofoam bowls with the spoons sticking out of the creamy blobs of vanilla cream. No one turned down the ice cream. Nothing tasted quite like homemade vanilla ice cream on a hot summer's day at the lake. It tasted like memories.

I didn't like how Jesse watched me. It wasn't like the Candy Man, but since then I didn't like being watched by any man. I wanted to get away, so I thanked Mamaw for the ice cream and went to look for Uncle Brody. I didn't like that he didn't get any ice cream. It was his favorite part of the picnics.

As I approached the bridge and started to cross, I didn't notice that someone followed me.

Uncle Brody wasn't at the graveyard. He must have circled back along the lake. I wasn't supposed to go near the lake unless Mama could see me. I decided to turn around. The graveyard spooked me, and I didn't want to linger. Jesse stood at the bridge.

"Where ya goin'?"

"I want to swim some more."

"You can swim right here." He pointed to the water below the bridge."

"It's not deep enough. It's for wading."

"You don't like wading? I like wading." He walked up to me and grabbed my hand. I don't know why I let him take my hand. I didn't like him. He led me to the water's edge.

"See right there? That's minnows. Lots of them. Look a there." I looked and saw what must have been hundreds of little minnow fish swimming in frantic directions. They didn't like us near their home.

He sat down and put his feet into the water.

"Did you know I have a little girl?" I shook my head. He put his hands on his knees.

"I sure do. She's a bit older than you are now. Fourth grade already. She grew up fast. Maybe I can bring her next time and you two can play."

I didn't say anything. I knew what could happen when I was nice to a nice man.

"Hey, do you know what I am?"

"You're Aunt Diane's husband."

He laughed. "Yes, but I'm also a doctor for children."

"You are?" I didn't remember Mamaw saying anything about him being a doctor.

"Yep. But I'm not a doctor for regular sickness. I'm a doctor for hurts in your heart." He tapped my heart and I flinched.

"Get your hands off her." Uncle Brody startled him, and he jumped away from me.

"I showed her the minnows, that's all. You scared her half to death, man."

"Looks like you're the one going to be scared. To death." I never saw Uncle Brody's face look like that. He looked at me, but I looked away.

"Tara, go back to the picnic area."

I didn't want to leave Uncle Brody there alone with this man. His voice sounded funny.

I walked up to the bridge but stopped to say something.

"Go on, Tara Gail." I knew I couldn't argue. I reached the other side of the bridge and then I ducked behind a tree, just like I did earlier when I spied on the black man and his son.

"Don't get all riled up and jump to conclusions. Diane told me about your nasty temper. Seems to me you'd learn to keep it in check. But I suppose a drunk like you wouldn't be knowing how."

My uncle stepped toward him. "You'd better go tell Diane that you're leaving now."

"I can't leave. Diane wants to see her kids. Besides, what are you going to do? Beat me up? All I wanted to do was talk to her. She's obviously troubled and needs some professional help. Something bad has happened to her. Maybe if you were a better uncle than you are a father, you'd see that."

Uncle Brody lunged and they both went down into the stream. My uncle dunked him over and over. He screamed and sputtered as his head went into the water and came up again. He kicked Uncle Brody in the groin and Uncle Brody yelped in pain, collapsing in the stream. He ran off toward the graveyard, but Uncle Brody recovered and caught up to him. They struggled back and forth and rolled around on the grassy graves.

"Look, man, I just want to help that girl!"

My uncle stopped. "I bet you do!"

"You're sick. Maybe it's you that did it in the first place! Maybe that's why you're so ticked off."

My uncle's face reddened, and he wrapped his large hands around Jesse's neck. He squeezed while Jesse pulled at my uncle's arms, desperate for his hold to release. Then, he kneed my uncle in the stomach. Uncle Brody lost his balance and fell backwards onto a tombstone. He didn't get up.

Jesse stared at him for a while, then kicked my uncle. Uncle Brody didn't move. "Hey, get up!"

Uncle Brody didn't answer. Jesse checked his breathing, then backed up with wide eyes, cursing. He took off in my direction, so I shrunk further behind the tree.

He walked back across the bridge and passed right by without looking my way. I held my breath, but once he disappeared, I ran to my uncle.

"Uncle Brody!" I picked up his head, but he didn't stir. "Uncle Brody!" Nothing.

I ran all the way to the picnic area for help, but I knew it was too late. I had the dreaded certainty that Uncle Brody had just died on another man's grave.

# 12

Uncle Brody's casket had an American flag draped over it. For the first time ever, I watched my papaw cry. He soaked his handkerchief through, so Mamaw handed him another one out of her purse. I expected my Mamaw to be the one to cry, but she just stared silently at my uncle's casket while the preacher preached. Like her, I couldn't cry. I had no right to. He died because he thought he was protecting me.

Everyone thought he fell on that tombstone because he had drunk too much. His drunken state only played a small part in how he fell that day. I knew it, and Jesse knew it. He had the gall to show up for the funeral. I didn't know if he really wanted to help me or not. It didn't matter. He didn't speak up about what really happened at that graveyard. He comforted Aunt Diane, who to her credit, seemed genuinely sad. Sam stood at her side, wiping tears, but Albert looked so much like Mamaw. Stoic and calm.

My secret screamed so loud inside me that the silence suffocated me. Guilt threatened to unleash my voice. Still, I said nothing. I was no better than Jesse.

David didn't come to the funeral, but he helped with the food when everyone brought it to Mamaw's house that afternoon. I had never seen Mamaw skip the act of serving food when people visited, but that day she just walked in, strolled through the hugs, pats, and promises of prayers, until she reached her bedroom door. She didn't emerge the rest of the evening. Not even to tell everyone goodbye.

Some of Mamaw's friends stayed anyway. They talked in the living room in hushed tones, but they didn't see me sitting in Uncle Brody's favorite chair in the darkened corner. It still smelled like him.

"That was her only son."

"He was always her favorite. Well, until he came home from that war."

"I heard he drank so much that's why Diane left him. Such a shame for those boys."

'I wonder if Diane will take them back to Kentucky with her."

"Probably best, but that would devastate poor Jake and Helen. That's all they have left of him now."

"At least she has Ellie."

"Yes. And her poor little girl who found him, lying on that tombstone with his neck broken."

"Land's sakes, what's that going to do that child? She's already a strange one."

"Ain't it the truth, though? Odd little duck, she was, and now this. I've always thought she was a dumb little blonde, but now I'm sorry for her."

"Now, Gladys, feeling sorry for her won't change her plight. We must pray for her."

"Yes, I suppose that's true."

I didn't know why they thought of me that way. I had never spoken to them much.

"I wonder why she's so quiet all of the time. She might be a bit slow, bless her heart."

"That's probably it in a nutshell. Oh, what the Good Lord puts on some of His best people. Helen sure don't seem to be deserving of this, but then, we don't know what He knows."

"You're speaking truth now, Gladys. It just makes me thankful."

"You're so right."

I couldn't listen to anymore. I sneaked out the back door. I found Albert sitting on Papaw's fishing boat by the tool shed. I climbed up and sat down beside him on the rusty seat.

"Are you going to go live with your mama now, Albert?"

He shrugged his shoulders. "I don't know. I guess if she makes me I will, but I'd rather stay here."

"I hope you stay."

"No, you don't. I've been mean to you all your life. Why would you want me to stay? Just because I'm sad about my daddy so you think you gotta say something you don't mean?"

"I do mean it, Albert."

"Well, anyway, it's not up to me. It's up to Mama and Papaw and Mamaw Webb. If I was them, I wouldn't want me to stay since I'm not really their kid."

"You're their grandkid."

"They'd rather have daddy."

"You don't know that."

"Tara, can I ask you something?"

"Sure."

"When you found him, did he have more beer somewhere? Like nearby? Because I thought he only drank two beers, but they're saying he had to be drunk and that's why he fell over."

"I didn't look for any beer." That much was true.

"It just don't make any sense."

I couldn't answer. I picked up a piece of a stick and threw it at the washtub that hung on the side of the shed. It bounced off the tub and back into the boat. I did it again.

"Stop. I want to be alone."

I climbed down and walked across the road to the Yazoo River. The last time I stood on those banks my Uncle Brody had swatted my bottom for scaring him. He had rescued me that day from an imaginary monster. The day he died, he thought he rescued me from a real one. I dropped down on the mossy, dirt by the water and finally sobbed for the man I barely knew, but really loved.

# 13

Delta autumns were just summers by another name. October's temperatures differed only slightly from the humid days of July. Albert and Sam moved to Kentucky with Aunt Diane and Jesse. I never thought I'd miss my older cousin, but Papaw and Mamaw Webb's house echoed his absence even louder than my uncle's. Papaw didn't tease Mamaw anymore, or anyone else for that matter. He didn't go fishing anymore, either. He just sat in his chair, reading the newspaper, or watching the news or football games. Mamaw spent all her time in the kitchen or at the hospital where she volunteered.

School had started so I couldn't see Onnie as much. I never even told her about my uncle. She knew he died, but she didn't know how it really happened. She tried to comfort me, but she knew something in me had shut down, so she backed off. Darren had gone back to Jackson with his mama. With my cousins and Darren gone, I played mostly by myself those days. Cindy and her new best friend went to my school, but they were in another class, so I didn't have to see them much.

A few days after Uncle Brody's funeral, David had moved out again. Mamaw told Mama she knew it wouldn't last. Papaw said he never should have moved back in. I didn't really allow myself to get used to him being there. He acted like a guest so that's how I thought of him. Mama didn't seem too disappointed. Not like last time he moved out. I wondered if she missed the preacher. I didn't want to wonder that, but I did.

Mama took me to the fall festival in Sidon every year. I dressed in a costume, usually something homemade and embarrassing, but at least I got to go. This year, Mama sprayed green hair paint in my hair, put white paint on my face, with black eyes and red lips, and put me in the same witch costume I had worn three years ago. The long, black dress barely covered my knees, but I wore black pantyhose underneath so no one would notice. My pointy witch hat stretched out and drooped over my left eye. I pushed it up, but it just fell again. With my one-eyed vision, I struggled to keep up with Mama as she took long strides through the school gym. Finally, she stopped at a booth. I pushed my hat up and looked up at Mrs. Martin. The booth had a jar of jellybeans, and we were supposed to guess how many candies were in the jar so we could get a prize at the end. I spotted the prize, a New Testament Bible, and I decided I didn't want to guess.

"Go ahead, Tara. Guess." Mama handed me the paper and pencil and I wrote a number on it, folded it, and put it in the box.

"We miss you at church, Tara." Mrs. Martin said. I smiled at her, though weakly. It was the least I could do.

"We'll be coming back. We've been going to my mother's church. She's been needing us since my brother died."

"Yes, we had heard. I'm so sorry." Mrs. Martin's soft voice assaulted my grief and clogged my throat with tears. She didn't look at my mother, but at me.

"Thank you. Well, I promised Tara I'd get her some popcorn so we're going to move on." She did?

"Am I really getting popcorn?" I asked.

"Of course. I wouldn't lie."

I swallowed a retort. We hadn't been going to Mamaw's church.

Mama talked with ladies she knew from work. I wandered off on my own with the tickets she bought me. I played the bean bag toss, threw balls at milk jugs, and bobbed for apples. After eating popcorn and all the candy they passed out, I wanted something to drink. I used a ticket to get a fountain drink and sat down on one of the benches behind the concession tent. From my spot, I could watch everyone at the festival. I saw one of my teachers laughing with Mrs. Martin. I didn't see Reverend Martin anywhere. I saw the man at the gas station who always filled our tires with air and our tank with gas. He had on his coveralls with his name on it. A boy walked with him, and they both held candy apples in their hands. I giggled as I watched a dog bounce around the booths, hoping to get a scrap of the festival goodies. Most had food in their hands and laughed when he jumped at them. Some kicked him away.

"Tara!" I heard someone whisper my name.

"Darren!" I jumped from my spot. "What are you doing here?"

"I get to stay through Christmas! Mama dropped me off again. Onnie let me walk over to the festival. She's going to pick me up to walk home."

"When did you get back?"

"Yesterday. I had hoped you'd come see Onnie."

"I couldn't. I had homework and Mama wanted me in bed at eight."

"Oh. Onnie said she misses you."

"I'll go see her soon. Do you have any tickets?"

"Onnie gave me some money, so I have a few."

"I have some, too. Let's go to the haunted house. I want to go, but I don't want to go alone."

"Cool. But are you sure your folks won't get mad?'

"It's just my mom." I looked around. Mama still talked to the work ladies. "She won't even notice I'm gone."

The haunted house drew the biggest crowd of kids. Noises drifted out from the large tent. As we got closer to the front of the line, we shivered at the moaning and laughing screams.

"You sure you want to do this?" Darren asked.

"I'm sure."

Kids stared at us as we stood side by side, but they didn't say anything.

"Where are your mamas?" the ticket lady asked me as she eyed Darren.

"She's talking over there." I pointed at her. A black lady talked with mama, so the ticket lady rolled her eyes and let us through.

By the time we exited out of the haunted house, I had screamed six times while Darren only screamed three. We laughed as we dropped down in some grass behind the tent.

"You were so scared, Tara. White girls sure can scream."

"You were scared, too. Besides, I hate spiders. That huge spider dropped in front of me, then when I walked around it, it moved and touched me."

"That was creepy," he said.

We walked around the festival booths and played all our tickets. Our last ticket we used to get cotton candy, so we sat down again behind the haunted house to eat it. I ignored the memory that came with eating the blue cotton. Michael Jackson's popular song came on from the haunted house and Darren and I started singing with it.

"Hello, Tara." Reverend Martin interrupted. His disapproving frown reminded me when he'd preach on sin and how he'd distort his face to match his distaste for the world's sinners.

"Hi, Reverend Martin. I saw Mrs. Martin at the church booth."

"Is your mama here tonight?"

"Yes, sir." The cotton candy's sticky sweetness suddenly tasted bitter on my tongue.

"Let's go find her together." He stuck out his hand. I reached up and took his hand as he pulled me up. I didn't dare say goodbye to Darren.

Reverend Martin gripped my hand so hard it burned from the pressure.

"Tara, you must be careful who the devil uses to influence you." Was he talking about Darren?

"Yes, sir."

"You'll be coming back to church tomorrow, so we'll be sure to get you back on track."

"Yes, sir." His tight grip loosened as soon as we saw my mother.

"Tara Gail, where have you been?" She didn't look at Reverend Martin.

"I found her with a colored boy, singing a song she shouldn't be singing."

Mama's eyes narrowed at him. "My Tara doesn't know any colored boys."

"I know what I saw, Ellie. Perhaps David moving back in has had an effect on her."

"David moving back in has nothing to do with anything." She waved at me to move toward her. The reverend let go of my hand. I darted to Mama's side and slightly hid behind her.

"Besides, he left."

"Oh? I hadn't heard." He looked around. "Ellie, we need to talk."

"What else is there to talk about?"

"We left things..." he looked at me, "unfinished. They need to be settled."

"Are things going to be the same?"

"You know they have to be."

"Then it's already settled, isn't it?"

With that, Mama turned me to walk in the opposite direction of the reverend and to our car. I turned back to see the reverend watching us.

He wasn't the only one watching. Mrs. Martin stared at him, then at us.

Just as I was about to turn back around, I saw two more sets of eyes on us.

Onnie and Darren stood together by the haunted house tent. Darren waved at me. Onnie didn't take her eyes off the reverend.

Mama surprised me by not asking about Darren. She told me to take a bath, then she retreated to her room for the rest of the night.

The next morning, we didn't go back to church.

# 14

Mamaw could cook just about anything except turkey and dressing. Papaw teased her every year that the dressing could stick to your lungs if it wasn't for the lumpy gravy she served with it. This year he didn't tease her. His hair shined whiter, and his eyes dimmed more and more each day.

Thanksgiving at my Mamaw's featured a family reunion of Webbs. Papaw's siblings, two sisters and a brother, and their families showed up, along with a couple of his cousins and their families, too. Aunt Diane and Jesse broke up, so she brought Albert and Sam for Thanksgiving. Albert bragged about his new friends at his new school. Sam didn't say much. I got the feeling he didn't like Kentucky. Albert probably didn't, either, but he just didn't want to admit it. The women congregated in the kitchen while the kids ran in and out of the house, annoying the men in the living room who were talking about hunting deer and whatever football team they rooted for.

Back then I only liked the rolls and green beans at Thanksgiving dinner unless you counted dessert. I filled my plate with pecan pie, sweet potato pie, and strawberry cheesecake. No one noticed because everyone talked over each other and clamored to get heard.

Uncle Brody usually talked the loudest about football. He shouted at the television, protesting in words I wasn't supposed to know when the referee blew the whistle at the wrong team. This year, the somewhat quieter living room mocked me with guilt. I couldn't stay in the house, so I pushed open the screen door and stepped into the chili November air. Albert sat on the steps eating green congealed salad. Watching him eat that stuff turned my stomach so I walked around the house to the orchard trees. I stopped. There, underneath one of Papaw's peach trees sat Aunt Diane, crying into her sweater sleeve. If she caught me standing there, it would embarrass her, and I didn't want to do that. I steadied my plate, backed up, and stumbled as the heel of my shoe hit uneven ground. I looked down at the flipped paper plate, which had smashed pie and cheesecake onto my blouse. I pulled it away to see that my desserts were still edible, but my shirt wasn't wearable. A giggle snapped me out of my dismay. Aunt Diane laughed, wiped her eyes, and walked toward me.

"Tara, are you still accident prone these days? I remember the time you dropped that pepper shaker and broke it all over your Mama's kitchen floor. We all sneezed for hours like we had a plague. Your uncle coughed all night long. I didn't think he'd ever stop cussing in my ear." Her laughter died away and she started tearing up again.

"Do you want some of my desert?" I asked her.

"Oh, no, sweet girl. I need to stay slim."

I had to ask.

"Why did you leave, Aunt Diane?"

"Why, Tara Gail, you sure are bold all of a sudden."

"I'm sorry. It's just that it made Uncle Brody sad, and I-"

"I didn't make him sad, girl. That blasted war did." She sighed and walked over to the water pump. Pumping some water into her cupped hands, Diane splashed some onto my blouse. She then scrubbed it with my napkin. It all came out except for the strawberry juice from the cheesecake. I guess some stains are just harder to treat.

—ele—

The next day I visited Onnie while Mama worked. It rained not long after I arrived, so she gave Darren and me freedom to rummage through her jazz records.

"Who's Ella Fitzgerald?" I asked, holding up the album cover.

"Why don't you put her on and find out? There's no better way to introduce you."

"You look like her, Onnie."

"Oh, child, that's a mighty fine compliment. She immediately reached up to touch her scar."

I set the record and placed the needle. The scratchy recording filled the room. Then, Ella's voice rang out and Onnie's face changed. She swirled around and danced on her living room rug. Darren and I watched in amazement.

"C'mon, boy. Dance with your Onnie."

"I can't dance." He shook his head.

"Can I learn?" I asked.

"You sure can. Give me your hand."

I laughed as we moved around the room to the beat of the music and soon Darren joined in. Onnie left us to finish her ironing. After Ella, we discovered Miles Davis, Duke Ellington, and John Coltrane. Darren pretended to play the trumpet while I danced on the rug.

"I believe you two would make a good duo." Onnie said. "Now come eat a snack. I have some peanut brittle and milk on the table."

I had never had peanut brittle before. Its crunchy, salty sweetness begged me to take another piece. Darren tried to dip his in his milk, but it just dripped off onto the table.

"Onnie, why did Mama say I can't go to Shiloh?"

Onnie handed him a napkin. "You need to ask your mama that, boy."

"I did. She won't tell me."

"It's because it's dangerous. Right, Onnie?"

"Oh, girl, I wish that were all. It is dangerous, but there's more to it than that." She sighed, leaned back in her chair, and stared at the ceiling. Darren looked at me and shrugged.

"I guess it's time to tell this story." She sat back up and pointed her finger at us. "But after this, there'll be no more talk about it."

We nodded.

"Darren, when I married your mama's daddy, your mama was just ten years old. Your real grandma had died when she was three. I don't really know how. Cecil, that's your grandpa, well, he never really said, and I never really asked. Don't know why now, but it don't matter none. The fact is your grandpa had moved into Shiloh back when it was a neighborhood much like this one. It used to be folks helping each other out, and just doing their best to make their way."

"Why did it change?" I asked.

"Well, crime, I guess. People in poverty resort to all kinds of things to fill that ache inside. It's hard for a body to make a way sometimes and we can get tired. When we get tired, we look for something to make us feel better."

"You mean like drugs?" Darren asked.

"Yes, like drugs, but alcohol and other things, too." She rubbed her face again.

"So, Cecil is Clarissa's daddy?" I couldn't picture that man being a daddy. Especially to a pretty woman like Clarissa.

"Yes. Oh, she was a mite little thing back then. So needy and ready for a mama's hand. I tried. Lord knows I tried, but Darren, your grandpa tried to feel better with beer. At first, he just drank with his buddies on the weekend. Then, it wasn't long until he drank every day. There were times he got up in the morning, drinking before he even got dressed."

"What did you do?" Darren asked.

"All I could do. I took care of your mama. Her daddy changed right before our eyes."

"Did the drink change him?" Darren asked. I knew better. Uncle Brody didn't drink before the war.

"No, child. He let it change him. You know that cotton out there? Well, it's getting soaked from the rain. That rain is beating down on that cotton so hard, you'd think it would fall apart and disintegrate. But what happens?"

"It gets heavy."

"That's right. Cotton is strongest when it's wet."

"But what does that have to do with Cecil?"

"Hold your horses, I'm getting to it. We're supposed to be like that cotton. Unyielding in our faith. So, when the rain comes, we're supposed to soak it in and let God use it to strengthen us. Cecil didn't do that. He had some hard times that, much like that rain, didn't let up. He got pounded with life, but he grew weaker. That's when it started."

"What started?" Darren asked. I waited for her to finally explain that scar.

"Your grandpa hit me the first time when your mama had turned twelve. I did nothing to provoke him. He just came in one evening and decided he didn't like my dinner. After that, hitting me became a regular occurrence. I tried to protect your mama, but eventually he turned on her, too. We lived like that for years."

"Why didn't you leave?" Darren asked. "Why didn't you take Mama out of there?"

"Son, I have asked myself that every day for the last seventeen years. That's how long it's been since I lived at Shiloh. Tara, that day you were there is the first time I had stepped foot in that place since I left on that horrible day."

"What happened, Onnie?"

Tears rolled down her cheeks. "I finally saw what staying with Cecil had done to my sweet Clarissa. She was sixteen years old and by then drugs had filtered into the neighborhood. She started hanging around the wrong crowd, so I feared she'd get into serious trouble. I tried to talk to Cecil about her, but he got really angry and started hitting me with a lamp. The shade came off and the light bulb broke so when he hit me again, he gave me this." She pointed at the long scar. "I ran to the kitchen with the blood pouring out of my cheek. I tried to grab a towel, but he reached me and grabbed my neck. I thought he was going to kill me. Still, I didn't fight back." She swiped at the tears.

"Then, he did something that triggered the fight in me." She paused and clasped her hands on the table. "Clarissa came in the back door. That's when he went after her. He picked up a skillet from the drain board and started for her. Clarissa just lifted her arms up in front of her face and shrunk down to the floor. That spunky girl I had fallen in love with turned into a scared victim. When I saw Cecil pick up that skillet and start for her, I grabbed the percolator of coffee on the stove and slung that hot liquid right onto his face. He screamed a scream I still hear in my sleep. I'll never forget the agony in that scream." She shook her head and wiped a tear.

"What happened after that?"

"After that, I grabbed Clarissa by the hand and ran out the door. We left everything behind."

"Where did you go?"

"My aunt, my mother's sister lived here in this house. She let us live here, but then she got sick soon after and died. She left us this house. It has been the biggest blessing."

"My mama lived here?"

"Yes, but she left after my aunt died. She moved in with some boyfriend of hers. She had changed."

"Was that boyfriend my daddy?"

"No, that was before your daddy. I never met your daddy."

We were quiet for a bit. I got up and put on Ella Fitzgerald again. But this time we didn't dance.

That night, Mama came home late. I fixed her a grilled cheese sandwich. She complained that I cut the cheddar too thick and that it hadn't melted enough. She picked up my plate with my grilled cheese sandwich and took them both to the garbage can and tossed them in. She slammed the plates into the sick, one of them breaking. We had lost many plates that way. I didn't move. When Mama had those moods, I often sat very still, hoping she'd forget me.

"Get up and clean up this mess! Do you see what you make me do, Tara? If you'd just be the kind of kid I need, then maybe I wouldn't lose my temper! But you can't do that, can you Tara? You stupid, ungrateful child. I work my fingers to the bone to give you a good life, but you can't even make a decent grilled cheese?" She kicked the chair back under the table. Her eyes hardened. I stared at my cup.

"Look at me when I'm talking to you! Who do you think you are?" She came around the table, grabbed me by the arm, and slung me to the floor. She grabbed a wire coat hanger from the basket of clothes on the counter and brought it down onto my head. Raw, searing pain blinded me from seeing the hanger come down again, but I felt it. She hit me again and again with the hanger and inside I begged her to stop, but on the outside, I just flinched at the agony. She threw the hanger down onto the kitchen floor.

"Maybe next time you'll think about how hard I work. You'll think about how good you have it here and you'll do things right for a change. Now get up and clean up this mess." She went to her room and slammed the door. I looked at the broken mess in the sink. I looked at my arms and legs and felt my cheek. Red whelps covered my body and face. I picked up the glass, threw it in the garbage and washed the rest of the dishes. After rinsing and loading them into the drain board on the counter, I walked quietly to the bathroom in the hall and looked in the mirror. My face looked like one of the masks I had seen at the festival. Swollen eyes and swollen red whelps with traces of staggered blood stared back at me. My blond hair stuck to one of them. I pulled it away and winced. I don't know how long I stood and looked at my wounds in that mirror, but after a time I turned away, walked out that bathroom, and out of that house as fast as I could. If I didn't get out of there, my mama might kill me. I ran all the way to Onnie's house in the dark. The night sounds spooked me, but my mama spooked me more. A lamp shone in the living room. I hurried up the steps and knocked on the door. I heard Onnie's rocking chair squeak and then her slow steps to the door. She opened it slightly and peered out.

"Land sakes, child, what on earth are you doing here? It's dark. You ought to be at home where you belong."

"Please, Onnie, let me in."

At my tearful tone, she opened the door. When I stepped into the light, she gasped. She grabbed my face and turned it, looking in horror at what she saw.

"Did your mama do this?"

I nodded and sobbed.

She held me and cried with me, saying over and over again, "I'm so sorry, child. I'm so very sorry."

Then, she soothed my wounds with a warm cloth and put some ointment on them.

"Onnie, remember the story you told us today? About how you ran away when Cecil hurt you and Clarissa? And how you came here to your aunt's house?"

"Yes, child, I remember." She rubbed more ointment on my arm.

"Well, I'm running away. I'm coming here, too."

She dropped her arms into her lap. "Oh, no, child. You can't do that." She shook her head.

"Onnie, you said yourself you should have gotten Clarissa out. You said you should have left. Well, help me get out. Please. Let me live here."

"Oh, baby, I wish I could. You have no idea." She wiped my tears with her long, brown finger. She brought my face to hers and kissed my cheek. "Times haven't changed enough for me to take you. At least not in these parts. Do you know what your family would do if you ran away, and they find you here?"

"You mean you won't fight for me?"

"Baby, it's a battle I cannot win. Don't you see? If Clarissa had been young like you, Cecil could've fought me and won. It's even worse with you, being white and all, and I'm not even your kin..."

"I have nowhere else to go. Please, Onnie."

"What about your grandparents?"

"They won't take me. They won't go against family. They didn't even fight to keep Albert and Sam from their mama and she's only their daughter-in-law. No, they won't go against my mama."

"Do they know about this?" She gestured to my whelps.

"They know." I got up from the chair and walked to the door. "If you're not going to take me, I have to get back before she discovers I'm gone.

"Tara, baby, wait."

"No." I shoved her hands away.

"Tara, try to understand–"

"I do understand. You sit here feeling shame about Clarissa, but you won't help me. You talk about God, just like the others do, but just like the others, you don't act the way you say He wants us to act. And just like God, you don't really care."

I left her standing on her porch in the dark.

A few days later, my mama didn't come home. She left a note that said, "Go to your Mamaw Webb's house. I'll be gone for a while, but I'll be back to get you."

# 15

I guess Reverend Martin did me a favor when he ran off with my mama. I liked living at my grandparent's house. Papaw Webb laughed again and teased Mamaw. He never talked about Uncle Brody and that was fine with me.

Mamaw taught me how to make tomato gravy, fried okra, beans and rice, and skillet cornbread. Papaw took me out regularly in his boat and I caught fish. Papaw and I scaled and cleaned them, and Mamaw cooked them in four fingers of Crisco. Every morning at breakfast, I'd read the paper with Papaw and drink coffee milk. Mamaw poured half coffee, half milk, then a teaspoon of sugar and vanilla. Nothing tasted quite like that contrast of sweet and bitter. The cup emptied all too soon for me.

I missed Onnie, but I couldn't go back just yet. I missed Darren, too, but I figured he had gone home. I regretted not saying goodbye and wondered what Onnie had told him. I guess it was silly, my staying away, but the sting of her rejection wouldn't allow me to mourn her absence any more than I mourned my mother's. As far as I was concerned, she betrayed me, too.

Aunt Diane sent a postcard. She and my cousins had moved to Florida because her sister got her a job managing an apartment building. They lived in one of the two-bedroom apartments as part of her salary. Papaw said we'd never see those boys again.

Mamaw shoved the postcard with the sunny beach scene into the desk drawer and retreated to the kitchen.

Still no word from my mama. I saw Mrs. Martin once not long after Mama and the reverend left together. Mamaw had sent me into the drug store for Papaw's licorice candy. Mrs. Martin ran the register at the only counter. She didn't look the same at all.

"Hello, Tara." She didn't smile. For the first time since I had met her, she didn't smile. And I knew why.

"Hi." When she handed me my change, I didn't look at her again. I couldn't face that frown knowing I had helped put it there.

Spring passed and summer swept onto the Delta fields with an intense heat wave. Mamaw and I washed her Buick in our swimsuits.

"Tara Gail, your mama called. She left a phone number where she could be reached. I told her I'd tell you. Do you want to call her back?"

I sat on the wet hood, soaping the windshield underneath the wiper blades. Mamaw stopped squirting the tires and waited.

"I don't know. Do I have to?"

"No. I told her I wouldn't make you."

"Is she still with him?"

"She didn't say, and I didn't ask."

"Oh."

"Tara, would you like to go back to church?" This new subject scared me more than the first.

Panic slammed my chest. Everything in me wanted to scream no and run.

"I think I want to go Sunday," she said. She didn't say anything else. She didn't really ask me to get my opinion, but to inform me we were going. Like everything else in my life, I had no say.

Sunday morning came as fast as the heat. I wore a sundress with slightly heeled sandals. Mama had sent me bangle bracelets, so I wore them on my left arm. Mamaw had bought me barrettes, so I put two in my hair, one on each side, and wore lip gloss. I examined myself in the mirror and felt quite pleased with my image. Feeling pretty, I scowled when I remembered where I had to go.

"Aren't you going with us, Papaw?" I asked him as I sipped my coffee milk.

"Nah, gal, I'm too old for that stuff."

Mamaw shook her head and cleared the table.

Freedom Baptist Church held about 20 members, most around my grandmother's age. Metal chairs sat in rows with an aisle in the middle. Green carpet ran up the floor and on the altar steps and podium. An American flagpole was on one end of the podium and a Christian flag on the other. On the wall a wooden board with removable letters displayed the offering and attendance for the prior Sunday.

Mamaw introduced me to Bro. Evans. The last time I had attended, there was another preacher. Bro. Evans reached out his hand to shake mine. I placed my weak hand in his and he immediately let go. His gentle smile reminded me of Mrs. Martin. Mamaw took me to my Sunday school class. There were only four kids in my class, including me. Two boys and another girl. One of the boys elbowed the other and lifted his chin when I walked in.

"Well, hello." Mrs. Simms, the teacher, smiled at me. She wore those glasses attached by a chain and her lipstick shone brighter than my red Christmas pajamas. She gave me a Sunday school book and told me to sit next to the girl named Amanda. The boy named Adam was her brother. His friend Jason had elbowed him earlier.

Mrs. Simms told a story I'd heard before about Joseph and the coat of many colors. I couldn't blame those brothers. Why did Jacob the father make one of his sons a special coat and not the others? It seemed to me Jacob should be blamed more than the brothers. Mrs. Simms gave us a color sheet with Joseph and his coat. I froze. The last time I colored on a Bible story color sheet, I had colored with him.

"You're supposed to be coloring." Amanda said.

I picked up a crayon and started coloring his coat of many colors. When I finished, I realized that I hadn't switched crayons the whole time. I stared at my picture in surprise.

"Look!" Jason yelled. "She colored the whole coat black!"

After Sunday school, Bro. Evans' wife played the piano in the service while he led the songs. She wasn't as young or pretty as Mrs. Martin, but her fingers raced over the keys, and she made hymns sound fun. Mamaw tapped her foot as she sang "Victory in Jesus" in her smooth, alto voice. Bro. Evans preached on the Israelites and how they turned away from God over and over and how God forgave them over and over. He said God's forgiveness never runs out so we should forgive each other no matter how many times we have been wronged. All I could think about that was, I could never be like God.

After the service, people walked down to the altar to repent of their sins. Some cried and as they cried, we sang. This church sounded different when they sang. More people went to the altar, too. The preacher talked to me like I mattered, just as I was. Still, I didn't like church. Church reminded me that my mama ran off with a preacher and left his pretty wife with a sad face. Church reminded me that some people's coats aren't colorful at all.

———

I finally went to see Onnie. She grabbed me and hugged me, and I cried. I told her about Mama running off with the preacher and how I moved in with Mamaw and Papaw. She popped some popcorn over the stove, and we worked a puzzle together while watching Little House on the Prairie.

"Did you know that there was a real Laura Ingalls?" she asked.

I shook my head, surprised.

"Yep. She wrote books about her pioneer life. Hold on a minute." She went back to her bedroom and came back with a stack of books. "Here." She placed them on the sofa beside me. I picked one up.

"That's the series she wrote. It's not much like the television show, but I think you'll like it just the same."

"You're letting me borrow them?"

"No, child, you can have 'em."

I stared at the covers in awe. I didn't have many books of my own. I loved to read, and during school, I'd check books out of the library. I didn't get to go to the county library much because Mamaw and Papaw only had one car and Mamaw used it mostly for shopping and church or visiting friends once in a while. I didn't like to ask her for favors since she took care of me for Mama.

"Thank you, Onnie. I'll take good care of them."

"I know you will." She patted my leg.

"Have you heard from Darren?"

"As a matter of fact, I got a letter from that boy. I thought he would come spend some summertime here, but he's going to some charity day camp for boys while Clarissa works. He likes it, so he said he might not come this summer, but he's going to ask his mama if he can come for Christmas." She sighed and tried putting an inside piece into a corner. It didn't fit.

"Tell him I said hi if you write to him."

"Do you want to write to him yourself? He asked me about you."

"That's okay. Just tell him hi." I felt so ashamed not telling him goodbye. I didn't know what I'd say to him. "Can we play your records?"

"Girl, you don't have to ask me that. My home is your home."

This time I picked out a different album. "Who's this?"

"That's BB King. You'll like him." She smiled.

BB King sang, and we finished the puzzle.

"Onnie, do you like any white singers?" I asked.

"Why, Tara, why would you ask that?"

"Because all of your records have black singers."

"Well, I guess they do at that."

"Why?"

"Oh, I don't know. Maybe it's just the way it is. I'm black, so maybe I connect to the music style. Or it could be I'm a racist." She laughed. I didn't really understand, so I didn't laugh with her.

She looked at my face and sobered. "Let me see if I can really explain it. You see, you white folks have a culture and we black folks have a culture. You like our music, right?"

I nodded. "I love it."

"Well, now black folks like white music too, sometimes, but just like us, you all have your own style. Does that make sense?"

"I think so. It's natural to like your own style."

"Right. I knew you'd get it. But I suppose that you all do the same, and that's why we shouldn't be so harsh with each other. Just because I don't have white music doesn't mean I don't like whites, and white folks that like their own music don't necessarily hate us. Look at those books right there. Laura Ingalls Wilder was a white author, but I love those books. You love this music. We can celebrate our differences and recognize them as good. Just as the good Lord does."

"Onnie, how come more people don't think like you?"

"Oh, I suppose it's just the sin nature of pride. Everything always goes back to pride." She got up and switched the record out to Ella Fitzgerald.

"I don't really know why people make relationships with other people so difficult to understand when the Good Lord made it easy. Love one another. The act isn't always easy, but it is easy to understand. No ifs, ands, or buts about it. Why they can't just follow the Good Lord's commands, I'll never know. But there's one thing I do know."

She sat down beside me and grabbed my hands in hers. "I sure have missed you."

"I've missed you, too. I'm sorry about before."

"Oh, no, child. Don't be sorry. I understand the pain that drove you away. Have you talked to your mama?"

"No. She calls sometimes and sends postcards, but I don't care."

"Oh, yes you do. Don't lie about that. It does no good to lie about what we're feeling. You have to face it head on."

"You mean I have to talk to her?"

"No, just don't lie about caring about her. Caring about her is natural."

"She doesn't care about me."

"How do you know? Maybe she cares as much as she'll let herself."

"What do you mean?" I crinkled my nose at her. Sometimes Onnie said the weirdest things.

"Well, sometimes people have something aching inside of 'em. Something deep and painful and they don't know how to address it, so they hurt other people. Even those they love. Sometimes they ache so much inside that they don't know how to show or practice love the right way."

I didn't want to listen to any more about why my mama didn't love me, so I turned my attention to the books. Onnie didn't press me, but I could tell she wanted to.

# 16

Papaw got sick after I turned twelve. Cancer took over his body fast. I helped Mamaw take care of him. Many nights when Mamaw sat with Mrs. Reba Johnson at the hospital I read to him. When I finished, he'd smile weakly and reach over to pat my hand. One night he didn't smile or pat my hand.

"Papaw, are you alright? Do you need some water?"

He shook his head, then turned to look at me. His cheekbones had sunk in, and his eyes had deep, purple shadows underneath.

"Tara Gail, don't hold grudges."

"Sir?"

"Grudges." He coughed for several minutes. I waited for him to catch his breath again. "You can't live life holding onto hurt. Not against family, and not against God."

I had never heard him talk about God before.

"Promise me" He coughed again.

"I promise, Papaw." I didn't know it then, but my words gave him permission to let go.

—ele—

Mama came home for the funeral. The preacher didn't come with her. She sobbed over the casket, wailing so loudly that I feared she'd be asked to leave the funeral home. Mamaw didn't cry. I guess I took after her because I couldn't cry, either. I heard someone say that Mama cried so hard out of guilt. I figured that couldn't be true because I felt an enormous amount of guilt. My last words to him were a lie and I didn't shed one tear. We buried him by Uncle Brody's grave. Mamaw bought a double plot for them when my uncle died, so her tombstone and Papaw's joined together. Their names were already etched in the stone.

Mama brought suitcases into the house and put them in my room.

"Tara Gail, you're too scrawny. How are you going to get any boyfriends when you don't have any boobs? And what are you doing, dressing like a boy?" She puffed on a cigarette.

I looked down at my Panama Jack shirt and jeans. "This shirt is in style. All the kids wear them."

"I don't care what all the kids wear. I care what my daughter wears, and you need to look like a girl. Tomorrow we go shopping."

She asked Mamaw for some money and we came back from JC Penney with dresses, blouses, and shoes. She also bought me a jewelry box for the jewelry she had been sending me.

"Ellie, how long are you staying?" I heard Mamaw ask one evening. I pretended to watch television from Papaw's chair.

"Oh, I don't know."

"Where is he?"

"Where's who?"

"You know who."

"Oh, Mama, I don't want to talk about him."

"So, he finally left you."

"No, of course not. I left him."

Mamaw didn't say anything. I heard her chair scrape on the floor and then her feet tap on the wood floor to the kitchen. I figured she'd rather attack the casserole dishes than Mama's lies.

Mama got a job at the local phone company switchboard. The house where Mama and I lived had been rented out, so she rented a trailer in a trailer park where ten trailer homes lined up in two rows of five. The owner had strict rules. No pets, no smoking, no drinking. Mamaw said if we had to live in a trailer park then that would be the best one to live in. She and I packed my room while Mama signed the papers.

"A child belongs with her mama. Still, I'm going to miss you." I knew better than to plead with her to let me stay.

"Will you be okay, Mamaw?"

"Of course. Don't worry about me. Besides, I'm thinking of selling the place."

"Selling Papaw's land?"

"Oh, I know. It'll be sad to let it go. We worked so hard here to keep this cotton farm going. But Tara Gail, you'll realize one day that sometimes you have to let go even when it hurts because it'll hurt worse to hold on."

I didn't really understand how staying in her home could hurt worse than letting it go, but I nodded anyway. The lump in my throat wouldn't let me object. Papaw loved this place. He talked proudly about his seventy-five acres and how he built this house with his own hands. He often walked through his cotton fields, looking out with a smile when harvest time came. I couldn't imagine not coming here for holidays. Not that it sounded like the holidays without Uncle Brody's booming voice and Papaw's teasing Mamaw or yelling at Albert. I couldn't believe it, but I missed Albert, too.

---

The best part of the trailer park had to be the proximity to Onnie's neighborhood. The trailer park was up the tracks a bit in the opposite direction of Shiloh. I could sneak off and visit Onnie and be back before Mama noticed I had gone. The worst part of the trailer park had to be Mama's new boyfriend. He lived three trailers down with a big Confederate flag in his window and a sign on his porch that read, "Beware of dogs and guns. If the dog won't get you, the gun will.' I didn't mind the dog or the guns, but I did mind how he and mama would sneak off to the bedroom thinking I didn't understand why. I didn't like his friend, either.

Stanley wore his t-shirts with the arms cut out and he smelled like cigarettes and beer. Glenn didn't drink, but he let Stanley come to his house to drink. Mama always made me eat with them, then I could go home. One night I realized exactly why I didn't like Stanley.

"Hey, Ellie, you know you got a fine little girl there."

"Leave her alone, Stan." Glenn said.

"What's a matter? I just said the girl is fine. She's a real looker like her mama. Hey, Tara, I'll wait for you, Suga."

Glenn laughed and swore under his breath. "You got no couth, Stan. Tara, why don't you go on home now? Here." He threw me a candy bar from the counter then sat back down at the table across from Glenn. He tapped his cigarette pack to his hand to dislodge another smoke then put one to his mouth. Mama plopped down onto his lap, and he patted her bottom. Stanley watched me as I left.

"Go on to bed soon, Tara Gail. I'll be over after a while."

She wouldn't. She'd be there until morning. She stayed over there on the weekend nights. Tomorrow would be Sunday. Even though church still unnerved me after all this time, I still wish I could go with Mamaw instead of sleeping in that trailer alone.

Sometime after midnight, I realized I wasn't alone. I smelled him before I felt him. Stanley. He pulled my covers back and climbed in beside me. *Not again.* He reached up my gown and pulled my panties off. I tried to fight, but his weight overpowered my small frame. I screamed for Mama, but he covered my mouth hard. She couldn't hear me anyway. She never heard me. No matter how loud I cried.

The next day Mama came in around ten o'clock. Stanley had long gone. I had taken a shower hours before and washed and dried the sheets on my bed. Still, my room smelled like beer and cigarettes. So, I took baby powder and sprinkled it all over the room, then vacuumed it clean. It helped with the smell, but it couldn't help the dirty feeling deep inside me. It couldn't help the anger.

# 17

Stanley continued to visit me until Glenn moved out of the trailer park three years later. Some days I begged God for death. Glenn and Mama eventually broke it off, but Mama soon found another man to take his place. Mamaw had sold the old place and moved into a home, but she died just months later. Everyone, even Mama, said it was from a broken heart.

I never told Onnie about Stanley. By the time I turned sixteen, I hated men. I hated my mama, too. But I'm pretty sure I hated God most of all. I still loved Onnie, though. By the time I turned sixteen, Onnie's neighborhood had changed. The city council had voted to restore Color Town. Although its name had never been official anyway, they voted to call the rows of houses Hinkley Town, after the colored man who saved a girl from the railroad tracks in the early 1920's. Onnie said they just wanted to improve racial relations and status, but she seemed proud just the same. They paved their roads, put sod grass in every yard, and painted the houses. Many poor white people complained that they had neighborhoods in disarray as well. Onnie said they needed to focus on helping all by doing one at a time, but she figured they'd only do what made political sense.

Darren finally came back for a visit. It had been three years since I saw him. He hugged me, then stared curiously at me when I slightly pushed him away. He teased me about my "stick legs" and I teased him about his mustache. He showed me a picture of a beautiful girl and said that he planned to marry her the following summer. He had joined the military and would be getting his orders soon. My heart fell. While I wanted him to be happy, I didn't want to share him. We had written back and forth, and now for the past six months Onnie shook her head when I had asked if I had a letter from him. Then I knew why. My best friend had a new best friend. Just like Cindy. I shoved that thought down. No, that wasn't Darren.

"What about you?" he asked. He folded his wallet and returned it to his back pocket.

"What about me?"

"C'mon. You must have a fella or two at your heels. You may be lanky and skinny, but you're a looker alright." He laughed. "For a white chick."

"Ha, ha. No. I don't have anyone. I don't have time for that." The thought of a boy even holding my hand gave me an inner shudder.

"Why not? Don't tell me you spend all your time over here at Onnie's. Onnie, don't you let this girl out once in a while?"

"Don't go blaming me for that child not having any boyfriends. She's certainly pretty enough. No, it's not my doing, Darren James."

"Well, give it time. You'll be like me before you know it. Married with a brood of children."

"You want kids?" I asked.

"You bet. At least three or four. You don't?'

I shrugged. "I don't know." I didn't want to tell him that I didn't plan on getting married. Ever.

Later, we walked the streets like we had done so many times before. "I'm finally going to do it, Tara."

"Do what?"

"Confront my grandpa. I want to meet him."

"Why? You heard what Onnie said."

"That was years ago. By now he might have changed. Maybe he regrets how he treated Onnie and my mom. I don't know. I guess I just want to connect to my roots before I settle down. You know?"

Funny, but I didn't. I wanted to run away from my roots as fast as my stick legs could carry me.

"I met him, Darren. He didn't seem too changed to me."

"How long ago was that, though? Anyway, it don't matter none. I still need to settle things. At least I can tell my kids I knew their great grandfather one day."

"What's the plan?"

"I figured I'd go today."

"Onnie won't be happy about that."

"I know. But I'm not a kid anymore. I'm nineteen. Old enough to sign up for the Navy. Old enough to get married. I figure I'm old enough to go to old scary Shiloh now."

"Do you want me to go with you?"

"Nah. I'll be alright. You keep Onnie company so she don't fret too much."

"I might have to keep her from chasing after you with a whip." We both laughed at the thought and clanked our root beer bottles together the way we did so long ago. They didn't quite sound the same as they did back then.

---

"I can't believe you fool kids. Didn't you learn nothin' back then?" She walked ahead of me, even though my legs were now just as long."

"Onnie, wait. He didn't want us to go with him."

"I don't care what the boy wanted. He and his mama neither one got no common sense. You neither, I suppose."

"Do you really think he could get hurt?"

"I don't know. No telling what could happen with that Cecil. Or that other riffraff that lives around there. Shiloh's gotten even worse now, baby girl."

"But Onnie, isn't Cecil old now?"

She laughed. "I guess he is compared to you. I guess that means I am, too."

"You're not old."

"Oh, child, don't try to distract me from my anger with your empty flattering. I've seen the gray in my hair and the wrinkles on my cheeks."

Onnie had changed since that day she saw me on the street and offered me "store bought" cookies, but she still walked with spunk and sass as she often called it. She still looked like Ella to me.

"If you're so old, then why can't I keep up with you?"

"Perhaps you're not as worried as I am. Urgency quickens a stride."

She was wrong about that. My stomach flipped in knots thinking my friend could be hurt.

We reached Shiloh just as dusk settled and the mosquitos buzzed. The dim light obscured our vision, but Onnie cocked the pistol she carried and slid it back into the pocket on her dress. Tribal drums beat inside my chest when I saw that shiny weapon in her hand. It was the same pistol she had pointed at Cecil years ago.

"Stay here."

"But Onnie..."

"I said, stay. Don't you give me no lip."

She walked the weedy slope toward the shacks. The little broken houses resembled the National Geographic pictures Papaw had liked to look at. If I didn't know better, I'd think an African settlement sat by that creek. I hadn't been by here in years and conditions had certainly worsened. Crickets started sounding off in the trees and the whippoorwill called in response. I jumped.

Nerves pushed my feet in motion. I knew Onnie would skin me alive, but I didn't like the ominous feeling welling up inside me. Something would happen tonight, and I needed to make sure it didn't happen to Onnie and Darren.

I followed in the direction Onnie walked and caught up to her shadow. I didn't want her to see me, so I lagged behind. She stopped suddenly and ducked behind a shed. I stopped. No light illuminated my path, so I just remained still. She didn't notice me. Her eyes zoned in on the group ahead. There, in the midst of several young men, stood Darren.

"I ain't gonna ask you again, man. What are you doing in Shiloh?"

"I told you, my grandfather lives here. I just wanted to see him."

"What's his name?"

"Cecil Farley."

Laughter broke out amongst the boys surrounding him. The leader took out his switchblade knife and slid his finger up and down the blade. I didn't know if this intimidated Darren, but it sure intimidated me. My tribal drums beat stronger.

"Cecil don't have no grandson. He ain't never had nobody but his drunken self. Know how it is I know?" He stepped closer to Darren. "Cause he died last year and I ain't seen you nor anybody else showing up at Shiloh. Now, why you here?"

"I didn't know he died." Darren's voice weakened with each word as the boy got right in front of his face.

"If he is your grandpa, I'd think you'd know. So, you know what I think? Either you're lying about Cecil, and you're actually here for a girl, or you're lying about Cecil, and you're here to score a deal, or you're telling the truth about Cecil, and you know where he hid it."

Darren frowned at him. "Hid what?"

"Don't go acting all innocent. Anyone who knows Cecil's name knows he stole a heap load of money a while back and he hid it. I think you know where it is." He put the knife to Darren's throat. "And you're going to tell me where, or you'll get your throat slit."

"I don't know where no stolen money is." Darren moved quickly, darting between two boys, but they grabbed his legs and he toppled to the ground.

"Hold him, boys."

Onnie stepped out at that moment, pistol raised and pointed. "Just a minute, boys."

All eyes turned toward Onnie.

"What have you got there? A 38?" The ringleader asked. "You know you ain't going to shoot nobody."

"You think? That's my grandson you got on the ground there. You'd better believe I'll shoot."

The boy narrowed his eyes. "You Cecil Farley's woman? The one that run off?"

"So, you knew my grandson told the truth."

"I knew no such thang. I just know that if anybody knows Cecil, they must know where he kept that money. That's how he got himself killed. He hid that money and didn't share it with Lonny Banks. Big mistake. Ole Lonny don't play around. Guess who Lonny is? He's my pop. Now, if you know where that money is, we'll let your boy here go."

"You'll let him go now." She cocked the pistol. "I don't know what Cecil did with money or anything else because we haven't been married for years. But if you've got my guess, he spent it all on booze, so let my boy go or you'll get one of these bullets in you."

"Hold on, now, woman."

"My name's Onnie. I ain't gonna tell you again to let my boy go." She fired at their feet. Curses flew in the air as their legs scrambled in a frenzy to get away from the bullet.

Darren jumped to his feet and bolted toward our direction, but the leader acted fast. He jabbed him high in the back with his knife and Darren fell on top of Onnie. They both went with a thud to the ground. Onnie got out from beneath him quickly and turned Darren over.

"Darren!" I screamed and ran to his crumpled form on the ground. Blood poured onto the ground. The leader picked up the gun and pointed it right at us. He pushed Darren with his foot. His face scrunched in pain.

Onnie bent over him, sobbing. Darren tried to move but couldn't.

Rage filled me at seeing the two people I loved, who loved me back, suffering. The two people who gave me a home. I lunged at the leader and grabbed the gun. We were about the same height, but he had me by about forty pounds. I wrestled with him, and he pushed me down, but the gun fell to the ground. I grabbed it, but he jumped on top of me. I felt the gun go off more than I heard it. The vibration went through my stomach and at first, I thought I had been shot. He collapsed on top of me, and I felt the sticky, red substance soak into my shirt. I screamed.

"Hush, Tara. C'mon." Onnie pulled me out from under him, but I just stared in shock. "Baby, c'mon. We got to go."

The sirens snapped me out of it. "Darren!" I jumped up and ran to his side. His eyes stared up but did not blink.

"No! Darren! Please, wake up! Please!" My tears fell onto his cheeks.

"Tara, baby, we got to get out of here. Now." Her voice sounded so far away.

"Onnie, we can't leave him here!"

"We have to. Tara, let's go. Now." She wiped the gun off and placed it in Darren's hands. She quickly swiped our tears from his face with her dress. Then, she grabbed me by the arms and yanked me up. We started running. We went through the creek. It was difficult to see where we ran because the moon hid partially behind the trees. We stopped there and watched. By now, people had gathered around the bodies, talking excitedly, and looking around.

"Those other boys won't be back, so we don't have to worry about them. They won't want the police knowing their part in this." Onnie whispered.

"Onnie..."

"We'll head back to my house as soon as the police arrive. We don't want to be caught on the street."

"Onnie..." I whispered a bit louder.

"They'll think Darren and the boy got into a fight. At least it won't be murder from Darren. Knowing that other boy's reputation, they'll think its self-defense. They'll be coming to my house soon, Tara, so we'll have to move fast."

"Onnie!"

"Shhhh! What?"

"Darren's dead! Don't you get that? Darren's dead!" I sobbed as quietly as I could.

Onnie grabbed my face. "Hush, child. There ain't no time for grieving right now. We'll have to grieve for him later. Right now, we've got to get outta here. Take your shirt off."

"What?"

"I said take that shirt off. Bra, too."

"What will I put on?"

"Nothing. We gotta run in these here woods until we reach the upper tracks, then we'll double back to my house. We'll just make sure no one see you.

"Onnie, I can't..." Police lights circled around the area.

"Do it now. They're here." I jerked my shirt off and then unclasped my bra. Embarrassed, I covered myself, not really knowing what to do.

Onnie shoved my clothes into an old stump and covered it with leaves.

"C'mon, let's go."

We ran all the way around the long way to the back of Onnie's house, making sure no one saw us. I held my arms over my breasts the whole way. Onnie said modesty had no place if it came before survival. Stepping into the kitchen, I noticed Darren's Navy t-shirt on the table. I collapsed into Onnie's arms, and we sobbed together.

## 18

We didn't grieve long. Onnie rushed me to put on one of her blouses and get on home.

"Onnie, I can't leave you to deal with this alone."

"You do not need to be here. They're going to come here to deliver the news. I have to act surprised and grieved. Although the grief part I can handle. I don't know what I'm going to tell his mama." Her voice quivered and she put her hands to her face.

"I'll go, Onnie. I want you to be calm when they get here." I hugged her again and left her alone in her living room.

I entered the trailer from the back door and went straight to my room.

"Tara?" My mama called from the kitchen. I heard male laughter and knew Ted visited again. Ted was a sheriff's deputy. Alarm filled me. I don't know why I got scared. It wasn't like anyone knew we were at the scene except for those other boys, and Onnie said they wouldn't tell.

"Tara?" Mama called again. Great. She sounded annoyed.

"Coming." I called back. I pulled Onnie's blouse over my head and shoved it into my dresser drawer, then selected a bra and t-shirt to replace it.

I entered the kitchen to find Ted's socked feet on the table. He played with one of those pegged puzzles where the pegs looked like golf tees.

"Tara, where have you been?"

"I was with friends." I had learned long ago to tell enough of the truth, so I didn't reveal a lie.

"What friends?"

"Just a couple of friends, Mama." The ache at the thought of Darren lying on that ground with his eyes staring up still made me nauseous. The same eyes that shined when he laughed and teased me.

"I don't want you out gallivanting out there. Next thing I know you'll come home pregnant."

Fat chance of that. If I had my way, I'd never let another man touch me. Ever.

"Leave her alone, Ell. She's sixteen. Let her have some fun."

"Then you can take care of her baby when she has one."

Ted snickered and went back to his game. His walkie talkie alerted him to an urgent matter, so he stepped on the back porch to take the call.

"Wash your hands and finish our dinner." Mama sat down and pulled out a cigarette to light. The years were catching up to her fast. I turned away from any sympathy and went to the stove.

Porch chops sizzled in a skillet. They had already dried out, so I turned down the eye, and transferred them onto a plate. I started a sauce Onnie had taught me to make that gave the chops a spicy, sweet taste. Oddly enough, it was one of Darren's favorites. My throat swelled and tears threatened to surface.

Ted came back inside. "Well, I've gotta run. Some colored boys done got themselves killed over at Shiloh. Dang colors. You'd think they'd have sense to get outta that slum and do better for themselves. That's what happens when you got no morals." He grabbed Mama by the waist and kissed her passionately right in front of me. Then, he patted her bottom and she laughed.

"If you get finished in time, come on back."

He winked at her. "You betcha, darling." He looked at me. "Bye, Tara."

"Bye." I had to admit, Ted had never been cruel or inappropriate with me, just not exactly appropriate in front of me. He and my mama had no problem with displays of affection, to put it nicely. It grossed me out and usually I retreated to my bedroom any chance I could get.

"It won't do ya no good, Tara Gail."

I stirred the gravy. I didn't know what was coming, but whenever she nit-picked at me, it served me better to keep my mouth shut.

"Flirting with Ted won't do you no good. He only has eyes for your mama. Just because you're young and perky don't mean you know how to please a man yet."

I couldn't take this tonight. I just wanted her to shut up. I stirred the gravy.

"Oh, guess who I saw the other day?"

"Who?"

"Stanley. Remember him? He was Glenn's friend. He asked about you. Said he might come by to see you tomorrow."

My hand stopped stirring. "I don't want to see him."

"Oh, Tara, why not? He's an old friend. Just because I don't see Glenn anymore don't mean we can't be friends with Stan."

"He's not my friend. You see him."

She stepped to the stove and swung her hand across my face. I flinched and my hand hit the skillet. Reacting, I jerked my hand back and it hit her arm. She picked up a spatula from the counter and started swinging at my head. I lifted my arms up defensively, but she shoved me against the stove and the skillet burned my back. I yelled out and pushed her back. I had never fought back before, but the evening's events sent me into a crazed whirlwind of physical manifestation. My back burned, but I ignored that pain to inflict some upon her. I hit her with the spoon in my hand over and over. She tried to get up, but she stumbled back down.

"Tara, stop it! I'll have you arrested!"

"Go ahead! I'd rather live in jail than ever live with you again!"

"Who do you think you are to talk to me like that? I didn't raise you to talk to me that way!"

"Raise me? What a joke!"

She jumped up at that and punched me square in the face. Pain blinded me and I swiped the blood from my nose.

"I hate you." My boldness grew with each word, so I said it again. "I hate you!"

"Get out. You think I don't hate you? Get out!"

I ran to my bedroom and gathered up my favorite tapes, clothes, and books. I shoved them into my pink duffel bag and headed out the door.

"Tara!" Mama yelled my name, but I didn't turn back. There was only one place I wanted to go.

Two police cars sat in front of Onnie's house when I arrived. They were still there. I couldn't show up then.

I walked to the tracks and climbed into one of the empty box-cars. I used my duffel bag as a pillow and laid down. I arranged my headphones on my ears and pushed play on my Walkman. I wondered what they asked Onnie and how she handled it when they "notified" her. I wanted to be with her, but I knew that wasn't a good idea. Since she and I had both been at the scene, we'd be better off staying away from each other for a while. But I had to tell her goodbye. I couldn't just leave her, especially when she just lost Darren and the police questioned her. I couldn't do that to her.

My mind filled with images of Darren. The day he bravely stood up to Tyrone and his buddies. The day he laughed as we ran with watermelons we took from Ms. Annie's garden and I dropped mine on my foot. How he shared his candy when I ate mine too fast. The night at the festival when we sang.

I'd never see him again. That ache echoed louder than the Billy Joel tape in my ear. Nothing could drown out that sorrow. Not even the pain of Mama's long-term rejection could override the loss of my friend. Onnie and I experienced great hurt that night. We should have been able to hurt together.

As I waited in that empty, stuffy boxcar, fear of the unknown gripped me. I hated living with Mama, but I had nowhere to go. I couldn't live with Onnie, especially now. If anyone ever mentioned seeing a white girl at Shiloh that night, I didn't need to be here to bring trouble on Onnie. No, it was best I headed out once and for all. But what could a sixteen-year-old do? I had read about girls on the street and what they did to get by. I shut my eyes hard at images of what I knew those men would want. No. No money could be worth that. I could cook, but no one would hire a sixteen-year-old. I did look a bit older than my age, though. My height and a troubled life helped age me. Maybe I could find a fake ID somewhere. Tyrone would know. He still lived on the same street as Onnie, so I could pay him a visit. But how could I pay him for an ID? He would want payment. I'd think on that for a bit. I shut my Walkman off and removed the headphones from my ears. Rolling over on my side, I wished I'd thought to grab a blanket to lie on. Although hot, at least it wouldn't be hard.

The next morning, a fly buzzed in front of my face. I woke to that sound and the sound of voices outside the car. I jumped up and pressed myself against the wall of the car, peering out.

"Too bad about Darren. I liked that kid. He was okay."

"What about that white girl friend of his? You suppose she's the one they said was there?"

"I don't know. Probably. The guy Darren killed was pretty bad news. It just don't figure."

"What do you mean?"

"Well, Darren had joined the Navy. He had no reason to go to a place like Shiloh."

"He went another time."

"That's when we were kids, man. He didn't have no business to go there now."

"What about a girl? There's all kinds of girls living up in there now."

"Nah. Not Darren, bro. He already told me had a girl. Quite a chick, too. Showed me a picture."

"Drugs?"

"Nah. If he did any drugs, it'd be weed or something soft like that. Shiloh folks don't play around with no weed. They do some real business over there."

"Well, I don't know, bro. I guess we'll never know now."

"Maybe not. I won't ask Onnie, though. She's pretty torn up about it."

"I tell you what. We find Miss Priss, we find out what went down."

"She's probably long gone by now. And she should be. Ain't too smart hanging around here if you're involved in a killing at Shiloh. No matter what went down."

"True."

They left, but I still couldn't breathe. I knew what I had to do. As I jumped from the boxcar, I looked under it where I could just see the outline of Onnie's front porch. I stared for a moment, realizing that last night wasn't just the last time I'd seen Darren. It was the last time I'd see Onnie as well.

I knew there'd be no time for goodbyes. And no time for a fake ID, either. I went to the gas station and brushed my teeth in the bathroom. I had One hundred and sixty-eight dollars in my wallet. I could bus somewhere and then have enough for one of those hotels that take you for a week. Hopefully, I could get a job somewhere without an ID. Fear almost pushed my legs back toward the trailer park, but the thought of Stanley and my mother steadied my determination to get as far away from there as possible. I passed Papaw and Mamaw's old place and almost lost my resolve to keep going. Then, I remembered something Papaw often told me.

"Gal, if you can just bend in the rain, you'll outlast any storm."

He and Onnie often said similar things.

"Cotton is strongest when it's wet." That was her go-to saying when she wanted me to look at the bright side of suffering.

I figured I'd had enough wet. And I didn't want to bend anymore.

# 19

I ended up the statistic I never wanted to be. Getting a job at sixteen proved difficult without a fake ID, even in New Orleans. My hope to be a chef one day in a Cajun Cuisine restaurant led me there. I stayed away from Bourbon Street and the like, but I had to stay in a shady part of the city. The hotel I rented by the week was what my Uncle Brody had called a roach motel. Still, it had a bed and a shower. I sprayed it down with disinfectant I bought at a nearby convenience store. The noise of the city scared me. Although the trailer park shared sounds from the close encountered neighbors, the Delta noises paled by comparison to the Big Easy.

But when those jazz sounds from Bourbon Street started drifting over at night, I found comfort in the trumpets. I could close my eyes and pretend Darren and I danced in Onnie's living room.

The second week I was there, I still hadn't found a job. I had some money left, but I had to be careful with my food. I bought most things in little side stores where no one would notice a vagrant sixteen-year-old. I saw a postcard with the Huey P. Long Bridge pictured on it. I decided to send that to Onnie. Somehow, I had to let her know I was okay. I needed to connect with her.

When I got back to the hotel, I scribbled my message on the card. "Necessary leave of absence. Wish you were here." I didn't sign it. I bought a stamp and mailed it. She'd know who it was from.

I lived off Vienna sausages, crackers, bananas, peanut butter and bread, and little Debbie cakes. Sometimes the Little Debbie cakes would be a meal for me. I didn't mind. That little hotel room gave me a peaceful sense of freedom I had never known. I job hunted during the day and watched television at night. No one bothered me. But I missed Onnie.

I finally landed a job cleaning a different hotel. I decided to go by the name Terri. They didn't bother asking for anything by way of paperwork. They paid in cash every Friday. This worked well for my situation. I only made one hundred dollars a week, but I didn't care. My hotel room was forty dollars a week. I bought my toiletries, food, and other necessities and still had a few bucks left over every week. That's when I walked the French Quarter and observed the city as a tourist. Sometimes I'd get a beignet and coffee and read the paper. I worked hard, but I enjoyed freedom for the first time in my life.

Until I met him.

Mark winked at me one morning as he breezed in and out of the hotel lobby. I often cleaned the lobby before moving on to the rooms. He had a Kirk Cameron smile with Ricky Schroeder eyes and hair. My heart leapt for the first time ever that day. I had never known attraction for the opposite sex. My experience with men didn't invite such feelings in me. One smile from Mark changed that. As weeks went by, this became a routine. He breezed in, smiled, and winked, disappeared to the back, then left as soon as he came. I didn't know who he could be or what business a well-dressed, handsome man had in the run-down hotel where I worked. I made it a habit to avoid getting too close to anyone because I knew being a minor put me at risk of getting sent back to Mama.

But one day, as I was pulling trash out of the front desk trash can, he came in and went straight to the back. I must have been staring after him because Nell, the front desk manager, laughed at me.

"Don't be setting your cap for that one, missy. He's all looks and no good."

I ignored her. I didn't care for Nell. She gossiped about everybody that worked in the hotel, so I did my best to ensure she had no reason to gossip about me. I moved on and started cleaning the windows.

"You missed a spot." I turned to see him smiling at me like so many times before. He had never spoken to me until now. Flustered, I said, "Oh. Sorry."

He laughed. "You never been teased before, Jaclyn?"

"Jaclyn?"

"As in Smith. You look like her."

I rolled my eyes. "Right."

"It's true. You could have been one of Charlie's Angels."

"I think you're crazy." I said, reaching up high to reach the top of the window. He stopped my hand with his. Surprised, I turned and his eyes blinked inches from mine.

"Maybe I am crazy. Crazy for you."

"You don't even know me."

"I know you, sweetheart. Right now, your heart is beating so fast because you're feeling something you've never felt before. You don't know what to do with that. Part of you wants to run from it, part of you wants to run right into it."

Shocked that he read me so well, I jerked my hand from his. "I have to get back to work."

"What's your name?"

I ignored him and moved on to the next window.

"Doesn't matter. I can find out." He reached up and grazed my cheek with his finger, then left me in my confused state. How could I feel those feelings for anyone? Those thoughts plagued me all day until I clocked out of my shift to go home.

Slinging my bag over my arm, I started the afternoon three-block walk to my hotel. The cool night soothed my spirits as the jazz music floated with me. This had to be my favorite part of the day. Going through the French Quarter at dusk, watching the performers on the street, working for tips in a hat. Trumpets playing, carriage horses trotting on the street. Smells of spicy seafood teased the nostrils and the stomach. One day

I knew I'd be working in a French Quarter restaurant as head chef. I'd live in one of those fancy homes on Audubon Park. I'd be rich enough to move Onnie here. I'd take care of her. We'd walk on the Riverwalk together and ride the trolley to the market.

"Need a ride?" His voice broke my thoughts.

Mark looked me up and down, waiting for an answer.

"I usually walk."

"Hop in, and I'll take you to dinner. My treat. Have you ever been to Vacherie's?"

I had heard that place was pricey. They boasted of fine Cajun cuisine in the city. I wanted to go in there so many times, but feared they'd kick me out with just one look at my jeans and t-shirt.

"I'm not dressed for that."

"We can take care of that easily. There's a shop around the corner. I'll get you something to wear in exchange for you eating with me tonight. You don't want to leave a man to dine alone, do you?"

"I guess not." He smiled, jumped out and opened the passenger door for me. He took my bag and tossed it in the back seat.

The shop on the corner didn't have many different styles. Only one. High end.

"I can't let you buy me something so expensive." I said.

"Oh, don't worry about it. The owner's a friend. She'll let me have it half off."

I peered at a price tag. Even half off didn't sit well with me. "Still..."

"Hey," He picked my chin up so I'd look at him. "Don't argue. I need a dinner date. Remember?"

I found it hard to believe he couldn't get another date. Or that he'd want me to be his date.

We left the shop after he picked out a sleek, black dress with very little to cover my breasts. Feeling shy, I folded my arms as we walked into the restaurant.

"Take your arms down." He whispered. "You're a knockout. I want to show you off."

I couldn't believe he spoke to me that way. It both pleased me and scared me. Still, I took my arms down.

I complimented the food, using terms only chefs knew. He noticed.

"You know Cajun cuisine, sweetheart?"

"Only a little. I hope to be a chef someday."

"Ambitious! I like that. Here, try this." He poured wine into my glass, and I balked at the smell.

"Go on. Try it. How can you be a famous chef if you don't know wine?" That did it. I sipped from the glass. Within minutes, he coaxed me to drink the whole serving of wine, and then another. My head swam, with the intoxication from the wine, but also from the intoxication of Mark's voice as he drawled sexy compliment after sexy compliment. I had never felt more beautiful and appreciated.

The wine blurred my senses so leaving the restaurant didn't register until he unlocked the door to his apartment, picked me up, and carried me to his bed. His hands roamed my body, and I became alert with alarm.

"No! Stop!"

"Shut up! You've been asking for this all night. Weeks, really. Just let it happen. Trust me."

I fought, but he overpowered me, and then I found myself enjoying his touch. He said wonderful things that made me feel valued enough to give in. He held me afterward until he fell asleep. I wrapped my arms around him and cried. Maybe, just maybe I had found what I had been looking for. But as I drifted off to sleep myself, I couldn't help but see Onnie's sad, disapproving frown, and when I dreamed, I dreamed of The Candy Man.

# 20

I t only took two months for Mark to get tired of me. But he wasn't finished with me. He had moved me in with him two days after our first date. I just knew he loved me. He shattered that illusion on Mardi Gras. His balcony sat on a street where one of the parades ran through. I laughed and caught beads and drank until I passed out. I woke to find a man on top of me. I screamed for Mark but spotted him on the balcony with another girl. She hung all over him.

"You didn't tell me she'd fight!" the man yelled.

"Just give her a minute. She'll calm down." Mark yelled back. He didn't even look at me but started making out with the girl.

"She'd better! I paid you good money!"

Dizziness in my head turned my stomach. Trying to keep from panicking and puking, I pushed at the man's large frame, but he wouldn't budge. He smelled of alcohol and something else. Weed? He unzipped his pants and that's when I passed out again.

From that night on, I was a prostitute and Mark acted as my pimp. He promised me I'd study to be a chef one day, but I had to earn it first. He'd pay for my school after I spent time entertaining his clients. I could live there free, eat free, get clothing, and enjoy fancy outings and restaurants. As long as I behaved. He brought visitors to me sometimes five times a week. I lost count. Each day became more blurred than the one before until I just accepted the lifestyle as mine. I drank sometimes to dull the pain, but I never took to it like my uncle did. Mark didn't care either way if I satisfied his customers. Other than that first time in his apartment, I didn't entertain any of them at his home. The hotel where I cleaned served as the hot spot for clients. Mark had an arrangement with the hotel owner. By the time I was nineteen, I helped find clients not only for myself, but for other young girls coming on board. Every day my life in the Delta grew further and further away, along with my dreams of becoming a head chef. Even after all he'd done to me, my loyalty to Mark didn't end. I craved his affection and attention and worked to please him in any way I could find. My addiction to his praise far surpassed the power of any drug.

I often walked along Bourbon Street looking for potential clients. I didn't dress the part of a hooker because I wanted to attract the right line of clientele. Big money. Usually men in town on business trips, away from the wives, ready to party with a young body. One night Mark dropped me off at a bar popular for such men. They usually started their evening there as a group, then moved on to strip bars where they primed themselves for a night of sin. Alcohol and naked women usually did the trick. My job proved easy at this point. I spotted the vulnerable. The overweight, the stressed, the ones who couldn't take their eyes off any woman who gave them any attention. That's when I moved in. Mark taught me what kind of flirting to use to first get their attention, then the follow through that sealed the deal. It took only moments to watch a married man struggling to say no, then suddenly cave to lust and pocket their wedding ring. I stifled the disgust with them, myself, and Mark to survive each day.

"Jesus loves you!"

A man yelled at me as I passed in front of the sidewalk where he stood. What he yelled was nothing new. Men stood on the sidewalks often, preaching about Hell and how Jesus could save us from our sins. I had heard it all in my lifetime. No matter where I ran, Jesus seemed to follow. I ignored these men all the time, so I don't know what happened that night to make me look at this particular man. I turned and looked straight into his eyes. The bluest eyes I had ever seen. They made Mark's eyes look common by comparison. He had to be about thirty, so much older than my nineteen years, but his gaze captured me. I had never seen a man look at me with that look. Compassion? Pity? I didn't like it. Anger slammed into my insecurities, so I flipped him off. He didn't flinch like I expected. Perhaps standing on this street had conditioned him to this treatment.

"He does, you know. Jesus does love you. You don't have to live like this."

"Live like what? How do you know how I live?"

"Because I've seen you here three nights in a row." he said.

Shame filled my face with flushed red. "Go bother someone else with your religious garbage. It's never done anything for me. Trust me, Jesus doesn't now, nor has he ever, loved me." I left Mr. Blue eyes to scout the bar. Mark waited every night for his money, and he'd not stand for being disappointed. I looked back. Blue eyes watched me.

The next night, he stood there again. "Jesus loves you," he said quietly as I passed.

"Does he? Does he love this?" I flashed him, wanting to shock that serene face of his. He turned his face and spoke to another man who also passed out gospel tracts. They bowed their heads. I reached the bar and ignored all the men. I only wanted one thing. The bartender didn't have to ask. He poured my usual vodka cocktail and I swallowed hard and fast. I repeated this until Blue Eyes disappeared from my mind. That night, I scored three wealthy men. Mark praised me and swept me into his arms and kissed me passionately. He brought me to his bed, but I didn't delight in his attention. In fact, he repulsed me as much as the other men did that night.

Blue Eyes disappeared. I didn't see him for two nights. Then, when I finally saw him again, he didn't stay on the street long. I couldn't resist asking the man he usually worked with.

"You mean Chris? He'll be back tomorrow night. Is there something I can help you with? Do you want a tract?' He handed me a pamphlet with stuff about Jesus, but I threw it on the sidewalk.

"No, thanks. Just curious about your friend. We had a connection if you know what I mean." I talked just as Mark had taught me. I don't know why, but I wanted to prove these men weren't Jesus lovers. I wanted to expose them for the liars they were, just like my mama did the preacher. Mark had picked out an extremely revealing and provocative dress for that evening.

"I'm sure whatever connection you had with Chris had to be innocent, Miss. He's not that kind of guy."

"Yeah? Well, it's my experience that you're all 'that kind of guy'". I sidled up to him and touched his cheek softly. He swallowed hard and backed up. I went in and abruptly kissed his mouth. He responded for a moment, then pushed me away.

"You'd better go now, Miss. I'm not here for that."

"You may not think you're here for this. But you are. Ya'll always are."

I determined right then and there to conquer this man and his goody two-shoes friend. If this man came close to succumbing, I knew Chris would, too. I'd seen the way he'd looked at me, just as all the others looked at me. I'd be sure he paid me to keep me quiet so I could still give Mark his money. The idea obsessed me, and I tossed and turned with ideas on how to work my plan.

The next night, Chris didn't return. Disappointed, I walked up to his friend again and discovered his name was Stephen and flirted like the night before. He sidestepped me and tried to hand me a pamphlet. I touched him and leaned forward with my bosom to give him a view. It worked. He was mine.

He took me behind the bar. As soon as he finished, disgust filled his face, and he couldn't look at me. "I never should have worked these streets alone. Chris was right."

"Hey, you owe me for this. Give it to me or you'll regret ever looking at me."

"I already do." He threw the money on the ground and left.

Next to my clothes the pamphlet he tried to hand me earlier flipped open to a page. A familiar verse stared back at me.

*For God so loved the world that He gave his only begotten son that whosoever believeth on him shall not perish but have everlasting life.* John 3:16

*Underneath the verse, large letters in red stated, Jesus loves you no matter what you've done. You cannot run from his love.*

Wanna bet? I thought. I picked up the pamphlet and shoved it into a trash bin.

The next night, that man wasn't there, but Chris stood in his place. Another man stood across from him on another corner and passed out the same tracts. I didn't want to approach him. I didn't want to watch his eyes fill with lust and the pamphlets he passed out fall to the ground discarded while he rejected everything he preached. Still, I walked over. Again, I had dressed as provocatively as always, and I wore heavy makeup.

"Did your friend talk to you?"

"No. Was he supposed to?"

"No. I guess not. Where is he?"

"I'm not sure. He decided to work elsewhere. Do you know anything about that?"

I should have told him. I wanted to watch his kind features turn angry. I knew that underneath that facade lied his true nature. I shook my head no.

"Would you like a tract?" he asked.

"No."

"Do you want to talk?"

"No. But there's something I would like to do, and I think you'd like it, too."

"If you want to talk about what's in this tract, then I'm here. If not, then no, I'm not interested."

"You married?" I asked. I touched his lips.

"No." He didn't move, just stared into my eyes.

"You're not married, you're on Bourbon Street, and you're standing here with me. Don't tell me you're really just wanting to talk about Jesus."

"That's exactly what I'm telling you."

I kissed him. He still didn't move. He didn't return the kiss, either. Fury held me fast and I tried again. I pressed myself into him and moved to kiss him again. He gripped my arms and pushed me away.

I didn't even see Mark until his fist connected with Chris' jaw.

"Nobody pushes the merchandise." Mark said.

Chris stood up. "She's not merchandise. She's a valuable soul God loves and died for." He looked at me. "You're much more valuable than this guy sells you for."

Mark punched him again. Chris fell into the street. People stopped to watch.

"Mark, let's just forget him. He doesn't want me. Let's just go. He really didn't push me hard."

Chris looked up at me, holding his nose, which poured blood. Mark could've killed him. I knew I had to get him away from Chris.

"I can get at least two in there tonight. I know I can." I coaxed Mark away from Chris. He put his arm around me.

"Babe, if you can manage two or three again at the prices of last night, you're a step closer to that cooking diploma." He pushed me to the door, harder than Chris had shoved me away just moments earlier. "Now get on in there and get us a good score." He sauntered back the way he came.

I looked back at the street where we left Chris, but he no longer stood there. That night would be the last time I saw him for a long time.

# 21

The day I turned twenty-one I sent Onnie a postcard with a return address on it. I simply wrote, "Still wishing you could be here." That wasn't true. I didn't want her to see me and what I'd become. Truth is, it had gotten easier to forget Onnie in this life I lived. She had become a distant memory, something to fold away and tuck into the corners of my mind, just as I had tucked away Mama and all the other memories of my childhood.

I missed Mama. It didn't make sense, but I did. I ached from her absence, but I ached at the thought of going back. When I left home, though, I had never thought I'd end up just as enslaved as before. I had a plan, though. I needed to get away from Mark. Since I had met Chris, I had been saving money and hiding it.

As much as I loved New Orleans, I planned to leave as soon as I had enough. A man I had met once told me he'd hire me as a cook at his restaurant across the lake in the bedroom community of Mandeville. Ed had bought a little hole in the wall but wanted to class it up into a chic place for the locals. He needed someone who understood the Cajun food experience but could also cook other southern foods as well. Although his offer might have been made in the heat of his drunken lust, I knew I had to try.

On my day off, I rented a car and drove across Lake Pontchartrain to Mandeville. During the thirty-minute drive across the long bridge, I contemplated how I could break away from Mark. He barely noticed me anymore for himself, but he did recruit me for many clients who still requested me. I had lost my obsession with him once I saw him for his insecurity and small behavior. The only thing I could do at this point was to get a job, move away, and change my name yet again. I could even dye my hair. It would all have to be carefully planned so Mark didn't catch me. Maybe since I was no longer his biggest asset, he wouldn't chase me down and bring me back. Maybe. Mark didn't like to be crossed. He especially didn't like to be bested. By anybody. I understood that I needed to make the cleanest break possible. No trails.

I found Ed's place easily enough since he had told me where it was. An independent bookstore and a yoga studio flanked the small cafe style restaurant. The bookstore had a large John Grisham poster in the window.

I spotted Ed right away. He rolled paint on a wall while a woman rolled on the opposite side.

He looked at the door when I walked in. He froze and all color left his face.

"Can we help you?" The woman asked. "As you can see, we've got a while until we're open."

"I'm here for the chef position." I looked pointedly at Ed.

"Ah. Well, did you have an interview scheduled?" She glanced at Ed.

"Yes, Sharon, she did. I cannot believe I forgot that. I am so sorry." He climbed down from the ladder and put the roller into the pan, standing up the handle against an unpainted spot on the wall.

"Oh. Well, Ed, do you want to handle that? I can keep going here unless you need me."

"No, babe. That's okay. I got it. It's Miss Sanders, right?"

"Right." I followed him to the back office. He shut the door and immediately turned with a red face.

"What are you doing here?" He asked in an angry, hushed tone.

"You told me I could have a job if I wanted it."

"I was drunk, among other things. I say a lot of things when I'm drunk. There's no way you can work here. My wife will be working here with us. It'll never work."

"Look. It's not like we had an affair. We had one night, and not a romantic one by any means. I need this opportunity. I'm trying to make a change."

"Well, make a change somewhere else because you can't be here." He motioned for me to leave.

"I'm not leaving without this job, Ed. If I do, then I'll tell her how I met you. I'm sorry, but I'm desperate."

He grabbed my arm. "Stay away from her. What's your name again? Terri? You stay away from her, Terri, or you'll regret the day you met me."

"Believe me, I already do. But my name is Tara now. I'm no longer Terri. Just give me the job and she'll never have a clue." My stomach felt sick at what I had to do to him, but I needed a way out, so I shoved the guilt down and lifted my chin.

He scowled in disgust and his loathing stare almost made me change my mind, but then I remembered why I came, and it seemed a small price to pay. Besides, it wasn't the first time I had encountered a loathing stare of disgust from a man. It was the perfect disguise for shame.

"You'd better be good." He reached into the filing cabinet for some paperwork.

Funny, but that's exactly what he had told me the night he had paid Mark five hundred dollars for an hour of my time. He probably thought that I wouldn't remember him. Fat chance. I remembered all of them.

On the days Mark let me off, I drove across the lake and searched for rental houses in the same area as the restaurant. I finally found one for four hundred dollars a month. Ed had offered to pay me a thousand dollars a month until I prove I could bring the customers in. Since I thought that fair, I didn't argue. I paid the deposit and first month's rent, then for two weeks I managed to take what little stuff I owned and drive it across the lake to my new place. Weeds grew around the tiny front porch, so I pulled those with my bare hands. It would have to do until I made enough money to purchase a weed eater or could hire a neighbor boy to do it. I looked around. Modest houses surrounded the tree-lined street, but the manicured lawns provided proof that the neighborhood was clean. I bought a few cleaning supplies and tidied up the rooms. Strange, but somehow that one, simple act instilled a sense of change in me. That right then and there I turned things around.

The day I planned to leave didn't start out so well. I intended to go as soon as Mark left. He played golf on Wednesdays. Nervous excitement prevented me from eating much at breakfast. He noticed.

"Are you sick? You can't be sick. I have a high paying client coming in at noon. He requested you."

So that meant a repeat offender. I hated the regulars. I'd rather take on a stranger than a regular.

"Can't you get Alicia to fill in? I really don't feel so well, Mark."

"No can do, sweetheart. He specifically said he only wanted you. Apparently, you impressed him for whatever reason." He rolled his eyes and shoved his last piece of bacon in his mouth. His insults always wounded me in the past, but not that day. Mark lost his appeal for me the day I met Chris. The thought of Chris still stung, but I dismissed it. I hadn't seen him since that night and probably never would again.

"Are we meeting at the hotel?"

"Yes. I'll be back at eleven thirty, so be ready. Wear something red. He likes red." He bent down and kissed my lips. I didn't respond.

"You know, Darling. I could stir you up again anytime I want. You'd be mine in seconds." He spoke in a low tone.

I didn't answer but stared through him. I didn't risk angering him. It wasn't worth a black eye or busted lip.

"In fact, you give him a good time today and then tonight I'm going to see what I've been missing. Maybe I discarded you a little too soon." He kissed me again and left the apartment.

If he planned to return at eleven thirty, that didn't give me as much time to get ahead of him. Still, he'd have no idea where I headed. I jumped up and pulled my hidden duffel bag out from under my bed. Minutes later, I wore apparel that "Terri" never wore. I skipped the makeup, and I pulled my hair into a ponytail holder. When I got there, I could chop it off into a bob. It'd be better for cooking anyway. I tore off a corner piece of paper and wrote a street address in Atlanta, Georgia with "Aunt Diane" on it. I crumpled it and threw it in the garbage can on top where Mark could easily find it but think he had searched for a clue. He didn't really have much manpower so escaping wouldn't be as threatening as those dramatic scenes on television. Still, I didn't want him to look for me nearby. If he thought I'd moved to Atlanta, he'd probably move on to some other unsuspecting girl. Like he did every year.

I took one last look at the place where I'd spent the last five years of my life. I experienced nothing but emptiness. I took nothing. I had come almost empty-handed and that's how I left.

My routine at the restaurant proved to be long and arduous hours with little pay, but I loved every minute of it, and didn't even think of trading it for the lifestyle I had before. I managed to stay hidden in the kitchen, which made Ed happy. He wanted to hide me away as much as possible. I had cut my hair short, and I wore very little makeup so even if Mark saw me, he might not recognize me, especially since I purposefully wore dowdy clothes. While not exactly the fancy restaurant I'd imagined in Onnie's kitchen, the slower pace gave me room to experiment. The customers liked my food so much that we had more customers than the tables could hold.

"Well, I guess I should give you a raise." Ed said.

"I guess."

"Let me ask you something, Terri."

"It's Tara."

"Tara, sorry. What was a talented girl like you doing there? You know, in that."

"What was a nice, upstanding businessman doing there? You know, in that."

He blushed and turned back to his inventory order.

"Do you need anything else?" I asked.

"You need to understand, Tara."

"I don't need to know, Ed. Let's just drop it."

"No. You need to understand. I just had a night of weakness. I love my wife."

"Like you said, Ed. You owe me a raise."

He got the hint and nodded. "It'll reflect on your next pay stub."

I left wishing I had chosen another restaurant. Maybe Ed wasn't a good idea. I wanted to forget New Orleans. Instead, I walked into a reminder every single day.

I still didn't have my own car, so I walked home from work. A church sat on the corner across from the restaurant. A Baptist church with a cross steeple and a lawn sign that displayed trite phrases and sometimes jokes. That day, singing floated out over me as I walked past. A choir rehearsal perhaps. I stopped and listened. Laughter rang when the music stopped. Men and women. Definitely a choir rehearsal. I shook my head and walked on. Same old story. Nothing had changed. Maybe even Ed went to that church with his wife. Maybe another man in there liked giving little girls candy. I shuddered and turned to walk again.

"I can go in with you if you want." I knew that voice. Chris!

"No, thank you." I moved away fast, hoping my sunglasses hid my face enough where he wouldn't recognize me.

"Wait! Hang on a minute." He caught up. "Have we met? Because you look familiar."

"No, I don't believe so."

"What's your name?"

"Why do you need to know?"

He gave me a strange look, so I figured I'd better answer if I didn't want to draw suspicion.

"Tara."

"Nice to meet you, Tara. I'm the pastor at Willow Street Baptist Church." He pointed at the building where the singing just stopped. He stuck out his hand and I took it. Strong, but gentle. "Pastor Chris. Hey, why don't you come on Sunday? We're not a big church, but we have a big- hearted family. Here, this has the service times. Just think about it." He handed me a card.

"I don't really go to church, but thanks." I handed back the card. He looked down at it, then back at my sunglasses.

"Well, maybe next time I can convince you. After all, tomorrow's another day." He grinned sheepishly at the reference to my name. "I'm sorry, I couldn't resist. Tell you what, I'll go join choir rehearsal, and you go think about joining us on Sunday." He smiled and walked to the steps of the church building. I watched him walk away. He turned and waved at me, but I couldn't move.

If he had remembered who I was, would I still be welcome in his church? Before I turned to go, I saw a man walk up to the steps. It was the same friend that stood on the streets with Chris almost three years ago. The man that so easily took what I offered when he had just been preaching against it. That man had no problem walking into the church with a Bible in his hand.

# 22

I found a letter from Onnie in my mailbox. I ripped open the envelope, then paused. Shame seemed to pour out of the envelope as soon as I saw her handwriting.

*Dear Tara,*

*I cannot express to you the joy and elation knowing my baby girl is okay. I have fretted over you day and night. Knowing your whereabouts in that city and what you could encounter while there, well, I don't know. I just fretted for your safety. It was hard enough when I lost Darren, but then to realize my girl wouldn't come through that door anymore to cook with me, to play jazz records, and just to talk, well, that just tore my heart apart.*

*I know you've dealt with demons, child, all your life. I know about demons, and the one thing I know is that you can't run from 'em. They'll catch up to you sooner or later. You can't run from God, either, child. He's always there, wooing you gently, like I told you. He loves you, girl. I love you.*

*Come home.*

*Onnie*

That was Christmas Eve. The urge to drink assaulted me violently, which was weird because I had never been an alcoholic. I hadn't even had a drink since moving to Mandeville, even though the restaurant had an endless supply of alcohol. I had to get out of the house, so I put on my denim jacket and headed out to the street. I found myself at the corner right in front of Willow Street Baptist Church. Christmas music filled the night air. A large wreath hung on the door and the lawn sign displayed, "Jesus is the reason for the season". I wanted to drink. More than ever, just to numb the pain a bit. I walked on to a liquor store not far from the church and stood on the sidewalk, struggling. Was this the first step to becoming like Uncle Brody? I knew he wouldn't want that for me.

"That won't solve anything."

I turned around to see Chris. He wore a long coat and a fedora hat, just like my papaw wore.

"What makes you think I was going in?"

"Weren't you?"

I shrugged my shoulders. "Maybe. It's Christmas Eve. I get it, you're a preacher, you can't let me do it, but I promise, I won't hold you accountable for my sins."

He frowned at my sarcastic tone. He looked at the church down the street. "I have a better idea." He took my arm and I reluctantly let him guide me back to the church. We got to the steps, and I pulled back. "No." I shook my head.

"I promise you won't have to recite the Ten Commandments or anything. Not on your first visit, anyway."

I almost smiled.

He gently nudged me forward. "C'mon. Like you said, it's Christmas. You might like it."

I couldn't believe it, but he got me to walk into a church service for the first time since I was a kid.

The last time a man got me to do something I didn't really want to do, I ended up a prostitute for five years. Still, as Chris led me by the arm into the church building, I didn't think this would end up quite the same way.

The church looked much like Mamaw's church had. Metal chairs instead of pews, hymnals lying in the empty seats. The red carpet had seen better days, but it softened the shrill voices of the women singing Christmas carols. When all eyes turned toward us, I almost bolted, but Chris pulled me to a seat and sat down next to me. He picked up a hymnal and turned the pages, then passed it to me. I took it but didn't even look at it. I knew all the words to "Oh, Come all ye Faithful". I felt a piercing gaze, so I searched it out. There, in the back, sat Stephen with who I presumed to be his wife. We locked eyes. He knew. He recognized me. He averted his gaze and pulled the lady closer into the crook of his arm. The man leading the songs called Pastor Chris up to the podium. After he spoke on Jesus' birth, he prayed while men passed out candles with paper holders to catch the wax. I declined the candle when they reached me. My hypocrisy only went so far.

Everyone held up their candles and sang "Silent Night", but my hands clenched in my lap, and I didn't sing. I glanced back at him, and he stared back. I jumped up and ran out of the church. I just couldn't sit there with all the hypocrisy. Or maybe I just couldn't sit with all the shame.

I ran down the street and stopped in front of the liquor store again. I'd have been better off if I had just gone in there in the first place. I started for the door, but a hand grabbed my arm.

"It can't be that bad." Chris said.

"What's with you? You think it's your job to rescue me, a poor lost sinner?"

He laughed. "That's never my job."

"I'm going home now."

"Wait. How about a cup of coffee?"

"Aren't you afraid of being seen with a sinner?" I cringed, knowing just how much of a sinner I was.

"I'll take my chances. It is the nineties." He held out his hand.

"Aren't most preachers married?"

"Most."

"Well, excuse my bluntness, but you don't seem like the kind of guy who would be single."

He threw back his head and laughed. "I don't know exactly what you mean by that, but I think I appreciate it."

We walked to the nearest diner for coffee. The waitress resembled Cyndi Lauper, with a pink, punk hairstyle, and bangle bracelets. Despite her attempt, she couldn't hide her age. Fine lines around her mouth revealed a woman close to my mother's age.

"You know, honey, you've got great bone structure and hair, too. If you put a little paint on that face, and let me get ahold of that hair, you could be a knockout. Like that Julia Roberts."

She twisted her hips as she rushed back behind the counter. She reminded me of Mama and suddenly I felt homesick for something I never had.

"Personally, I think your hair and makeup are fine."

"I don't like high maintenance."

"Neither do I." Cindy Lauper brought our coffees and I watched him stir six packs of sugar into his mug. Grimacing, I took a sip of mine.

"Is that face because the coffee's bad or because you don't like the idea of my syrup?" he teased.

"I'm afraid it's both."

"I've seen you before, you know." I froze. The tribal drums returned in my chest.

"What do you mean?"

"At that new restaurant over there. I know Ed, the owner. I saw you come out to meet some customers on opening night."

I exhaled relief. "Yes, I'm the chef there. Well, me and a couple of other guys."

"I gathered that. Great food, by the way. I think the place is a new hit around here. We needed something different, too. So where are you from?"

"Listen, I appreciate the coffee, really, but I have to go."

"On Christmas Eve? Do you have family coming in, or are you headed to family?"

No doubt my mama had some man over right now. "No family. Just me and some VHS movies in my trusty VCR."

He frowned. "Are you serious? Oh, no. That won't do. You have to come to my parent's house."

"No."

"C'mon. I need someone to carry on my arm so my mom will get off my back about getting married and giving her some grandchildren. You'll be doing me a favor. Really." His blue eyes sparkled and sent my stomach swirling. He didn't affect me the way Mark did when I first met him. No, it was much more than physical. His character drew me like a magnet, but I refused to be pulled.

"No, sorry. I think I'll just rest tomorrow. The next day we'll be really busy."

He looked genuinely disappointed. "Okay, I understand." He paid the bill and we parted ways. No mention of seeing me again. It shouldn't have made me sad, but as he walked in the opposite direction, I couldn't help but feel I'd just spoiled his Christmas Eve night. And mine.

I watched him walk for a bit, then turned to go. I slammed into a chest. "Excuse me!" I blurted out but stopped as soon as I saw who it was. Him. Chris' friend Stephen.

"What are you doing here? In my town?"

"I'm not here to bother you. I just want to be left alone."

"Doesn't look that way to me. Leave Pastor Chris alone or I'll tell him who you really are."

"Are you going to tell him how you really know me, too? And what about your wife?"

He grabbed me and pulled me behind a pickup truck. Pressing himself against me, he groaned and kissed me. In disgust, he backed up, wiping his mouth. "I hate you, you know."

"No, you don't. You hate yourself." I said.

He scoffed. "You should know." He turned around and left me with that truth.

When I got home, I finally penned a letter to Onnie.

*Dear Onnie,*

*You're wrong. I know you want me to believe what you tell me about God, but you couldn't be more wrong. God doesn't now, nor has he ever, loved me. Do yourself a favor and forget me. If you knew me today, you'd be like everyone else. You'd want to forget me, too.*

*I do love you, Onnie, but I don't belong with you. I don't belong anywhere.*

*I have no home.*

*Tara*

# 23

I didn't understand why, but Chris waited for me every night when I got off from the restaurant.

He showed up New Year's Eve night to walk me home.

"A beautiful lady needs an escort home on a dangerous night like tonight."

"Shouldn't you be hosting a Bible study or something?"

"Preachers have lives, too, you know."

"Oh, yeah. I know." Images of Mama and Reverend Martin in her bedroom flashed through my mind.

"Curious." He said, watching me. "Something you'd like to talk about?"

"No. Now, look, I think you're nice and all, but..."

"Here it comes. You know we preachers get our feelings hurt, too. You're not giving me the 'let's be friends' speech already, are you?"

"Not even that. I'm sorry, but can't you go evangelize someone else?"

"Ah. Thought so. I suspected earlier you have a bit of a bitter church history, am I right?"

"No. I just want to be left alone."

"No, you don't. No one really wants to be left alone. They just say that when they're scared of being hurt." He reached out and grabbed my hand.

"You know nothing about me. I could be an ax- murdering psychopath, or like that woman from Fatal Attraction."

"Yep. You could. But you're not." He grinned. He pulled me close and kissed me. I couldn't move. Just a few nights before, his friend from his church did the same. Men were all the same. Except, as he moved his lips over mine, I felt a tenderness I had never felt from a man. I remembered the night I kissed him on the street, and he didn't move. He had showed great restraint that night when others had fallen for less.

He pulled back suddenly and searched my eyes. "Are you sure I don't know you?"

"Of course not." I worked to hold the panic out of my eyes.

Seconds seemed like an hour while he looked at me. Then, he pulled me to him again and hugged me.

"I believe this is where I leave you. I really shouldn't be kissing you, you know."

"You don't know the half of it," I whispered.

He cocked his head to the side and searched my eyes. Then, he tucked my hair behind my ear and whispered, "Goodnight, Tara."

I said nothing as I watched him walk away. Did he know who I was?

Apparently, I had panicked over nothing. Chris never mentioned me being familiar again. He just showed up at the restaurant and walked me home. He didn't kiss me on the lips again, either. We just talked. Sometimes he'd take me to coffee, sometimes to dinner, but we always talked. I don't know why I went along with it. Despite being drawn to him, I knew it to be a bad idea, especially his connection to my past, not to mention his friend. He never tried to entice me to another church service until Easter Sunday. One night he didn't show up at the restaurant. Disappointed, I walked home alone. In front of my door a giant Easter basket stood tall enough to block my doorbell. A card stuck out with my name on it. I opened it and it said, Open the egg. I reached into the basket and pulled out the large, plastic egg. A piece of paper fell at my feet. I reached down to pick it up.

*Let's have our real first date. A church wide, community Easter egg hunt. You can help me hide the eggs for 15 kids. Now, look at the ribbon on the bunny's neck.*

I picked up the bunny and the read the ribbon.

He had written his phone number in large, bold numbers down the pink ribbon.

I grinned and brought the basket into the house. Setting it on the counter, I dialed Chris.

"Okay, you win. I'll go."

I bought a white lacy dress with a wide, ribbon belt. I wore sandals on my feet and pearls on my neck and wrist. Chris whistled when he picked me up that morning.

"Sweetheart, you certainly don't need an Easter bonnet." He kissed my cheek briefly.

If Mark had seen me at that moment, he'd never have believed it. I looked far from the part of Terri on Bourbon Street.

After the service, Stephen didn't take his eyes off me, but his look didn't show the admiration Chris' had. He loathed me. Even if Mark wouldn't have recognized me, Stephen certainly had and wasn't likely to forget. Out on the grounds, I did my best to avoid being in the same circles as him. I should have been used to running into men I had been with. After all, I worked at the restaurant with Ed every day. But at church it seemed vastly different. I might as well have had a Scarlet A on my chest. Many ladies introduced themselves, and I shyly responded to their questions about the restaurant. Whenever they asked about my family, I told them my parents had been deceased for several years. After deviled eggs, ham, and potato salad in the fellowship hall, the kids started begging for the egg hunt.

Chris and I hid the eggs for the kids while they played games with the other adults inside. The church property didn't have a lot of grass, so we hid most of them in the parking lot around the cars.

"Okay, you have to remember where we hid these, or we might have a mushed-up mess when everyone leaves today."

I half-smiled.

"Do you ever laugh, Tara?"

"Of course, I laugh."

"I've never seen you laugh. A half-smile maybe, like just now, but never a laugh."

I looked down at the white wicker basket where one egg remained.

"We'd better finish. The kids are waiting."

"I want to make you laugh first."

"Chris, c'mon."

"There's only one sure way to do that." He pushed me to the car and started tickling my ribs. I squealed and dropped the basket, laughing involuntarily.

"I knew it. Sounds like music." He leaned in and smiled. We shared a tender moment before an angry voice surprised us.

"What are you doing, Chris? This is church property. You're our pastor and you're out here...there's kids in there!"

"We weren't doing anything wrong, Stephen."

"That's not what it looked like to me."

"Well, we can talk about that, but you know me. You know I am careful."

"Yeah, I know. Even with her. No matter what she tried, she couldn't break the saintly Chris," he spat.

"What's that supposed to mean?" He looked at me and I shut my eyes because I knew what was coming.

"Ask her. Don't you recognize the Bourbon street queen? Different hair, different clothes, and makeup, but look closely, Chris. It's her."

I opened my eyes. Chris' face first showed confusion, but then understanding dawned in his eyes. Then, shock. "You're her." He pulled away and looked me up and down. I turned away. I couldn't bear to see disappointment in his eyes. Or disgust.

"You need to leave." Stephen said. "Now."

"Stephen, leave us a minute."

"No. I can't leave you with a —."

"Watch it. Didn't you just remind me we're in a church parking lot?"

I couldn't take it anymore. I had to react. He was just one more man in a long line of abusers and I wanted to expose him for what he was. Even in a church parking lot.

"Why don't you tell him how you remember me so well?"

"Shut your mouth."

"Go on. Tell him what happened after he left that night."

"I said, 'shut up'." He started for me, but Chris stepped in front of me.

"What's she talking about?"

"Nothing. She's a liar."

"Tell him all about our encounter behind the bar and how you paid me."

"I said, 'shut up'!"

Chris stepped away from both of us, holding up his hands, his face ashen. "I can't do this. Both of you need to go."

"Pastor Chris? Are ya'll ready?" One of the ladies called out.

"Almost!" he yelled. His voice sounded normal until he turned back to me. "Well, Tara, if that's even your real name. I guess now I know why you seemed so familiar to me."

I nodded. I started to speak, but I knew things had not changed for me at all. I had no voice in this.

I left and walked past the curious glances as the adults accompanied the children down the steps. Someone called my name, but I kept walking. She called my name again, so I turned back.

"You forgot your purse." She said, holding it out to me. It was Stephen's wife.

"Oh. Thank you."

"Are you okay, Tara? Are you sick? Is that why you're leaving? Our house is just over there. You could come over and rest a bit."

"No, thank you. I have to go."

She looked concerned but turned back to walk to the parking lot. To her husband at church.

Funny. I watched her as she departed, and I couldn't help but notice how much she reminded me of another sweet, gentle wife who had offered me kindness. I no longer wondered how many of me were in the world. I wondered how many Mrs. Martins there were.

Chris didn't show up at the restaurant anymore. I didn't expect him to, but it still cut me. Business boomed, so Ed had planned to open another location in New Orleans. He asked me to go. The offer tempted me. I could make connections in the business. Maybe I'd finally be able to cook in the French Quarter like I'd always wanted. Still, I could run into Mark, or even old clients.

"Tara, I know what you're thinking, but you're the best person for the job." He told me one night after everyone else had left.

"Ed, you just want me out of here. I'm not exactly your favorite person."

"No, but I know that's not your fault. I just can't..."

"I know." I sighed. He made me uncomfortable when my old life came up. "It's not the best situation for me, either. I just had no other options at the time."

"Look, I can ask around and see if Mark still runs his network there. If not, then you're probably safe. You'll be back in the kitchen most of the time, and with the new look, no one will recognize you."

"You did."

He ran his hand over his face. "True. Just think on it a couple of days and let me know."

That night, I checked my mailbox and found a letter from Onnie's address. I cringed, knowing I had hurt her with my letter. I slowly opened the envelope, unsure what she'd say to me.

*Dear Tara,*

*You might not remember me, but I'm Darren's mama Clarissa. We met a couple of times. Well, Onnie's really sick, and she wanted me to write to you so you might think about seeing her. Also, I wanted to thank you for being with my boy that night. He thought the world of you, which I admit surprised me. White people ain't never had no use for us, and we ain't never had no use for them, but Onnie, she says you're not white people, you're just people, and I suppose she's right.*

*Anyway, I hope you get this, and I hope you do come see her. She never asks me for anything, but she asked me to write this here letter.*

*Clarissa*

## 24

The Delta hadn't changed much in eight years. Flat land with miles of cotton stretched over muddy fields surrounding the roads. I got off the bus at the small stop outside the store. Little black boys walked barefoot on the tracks. Inside the store, I used the restroom and bought a soda at the very spot Darren and I used to get our root beer. They didn't have those bottles with the bottle caps to pop off. I didn't like the new plastic bottles, but the cola tasted good. Just for sentiment, I bought a bag of peanuts and poured them into the bottom and turned it up again. Nostalgia hit me hard, and I almost cried at the thought of my old friend. I didn't like to think of how he'd look at me now.

I noticed the trees around the train tracks had really grown up. I started toward Onnie's house, thinking I'd better see her and get out of there as fast as I could. Locusts sang as I walked. I bent down and picked up a rusty spike, remembering how Albert, Sam and I fought over them once upon a time. I had often wondered where my cousins lived now. I had to admit that I missed them. Funny how I had thought Albert to be so mean during those days, but now I looked on those times fondly. I'd have given anything for one more day of barrel racing or digging holes to see if we could find the devil. I could certainly tell him that the devil had found me.

I reached the street where Onnie lived. It did look different. The houses that had been updated and renovated only a decade before had already fallen into disrepair. Even Onnie's. No plants decorated the porch. The paint peeled from the house and a shutter fell crooked from the front window.

Nervous, I approached the torn screen door and knocked. Footsteps echoed on the other side.

"Yes?" Clarissa answered the door. She didn't look like the beautiful woman I knew. She still wore jewelry, but her face sagged with wrinkles and her hair had gray strands at the temple. She wore no makeup or flashy clothes.

"Clarissa? It's me, Tara."

"Tara! Look how grown you are!" She opened the door. "Come on in, honey child." She pulled my hand until I stood in a living room that should have been as familiar to me as my own, but the room didn't look like Onnie's living room. The worn couch and chair had tears in the fabric. Cobwebs clung to the coffee table and to the corners of the room.

"Aren't you the looker now?" Clarissa shook her head, looking me up and down.

"Where is she?" I asked.

"She's in the bedroom. She ain't so good now. She done had a stroke and it messed up her speech and walking. Also, she has a bad heart. Doctor told her she can't do much anymore. That's why I'm here."

Dear sweet Onnie, I thought. How could this have happened to such a kindhearted woman?

I followed Clarissa to Onnie's bedroom. The blinds covered the only window in the room so I had to adjust my eyes to see inside the dark room. It took only seconds to see her. I couldn't believe the woman I saw eight years ago, the one that had stood up for Darren with a gun, laid there frail and helpless, with labored breathing and an oxygen machine beside her bed.

"I'll leave you two alone." Clarissa left and shut the door.

I walked over to the chair beside her bed and reached for her slim, long fingers. I pressed her hand between my two palms and patted.

"Onnie." I whispered.

Her eyelids fluttered open, and she looked at the ceiling.

"Onnie." I said again.

She turned toward me, and her face lit up. "Ta—" she said.

My heart broke. "Hi, Onnie." Tears fell from my eyes.

She shook her head. "No."

I wiped my eyes. "Okay, Onnie. No crying." She patted my hand. Then she pointed at my hair.

"Ha—" she said.

"Yes, I cut it."

She smiled and nodded. Then, she frowned. "Ta—sad."

"No, Onnie, I'm okay."

She shook her head again. "Sad."

I had never been able to fool her about my emotions.

"You're right. I am sad, Onnie. I have missed you. I should have been here."

She shook her head. "No."

I didn't argue with her. Instead, I told her about my job. I left out everything from New Orleans except my first job. I told her I made a connection at the hotel which landed me in Mandeville. I still knew to tell enough of the truth to try to make it convincing.

She looked at me a long moment, then leaned her head back against her pillow and shut her eyes.

Over the next two days, I learned that she needed those rest breaks because any interaction tired her out. I cleaned the house and fixed the broken window shutter. I walked to the hardware store and bought some paint and some fresh plants. I restored the front to look just as it did the day I met Onnie. Clarissa had to work at the grocery store during the day, so I made myself useful. I cooked some of my favorite dishes and did my best to get Onnie to eat. She did. Some. After three days, Clarissa had a day off and told me to go see my family. I didn't tell her I had no one to see. I needed to get out.

I walked over the tracks. I didn't even look in the direction of Shiloh. I couldn't go back there. Ever. I walked through the cotton fields toward my papaw's property. I looked across the road and saw the Yazoo River and the spot where I picked muscadines with Albert. When I reached the clearing, my heart sank. The house crumbled where it stood. No amount of paint or plants could restore the little broken-down structure in front of me. Weeds overtook the porch; the windows were broken, and the roof caved in. A tree had gone right through it. I walked up to the porch and tested the weight of one foot on it. When the board didn't move, I brought the other foot down carefully. I edged my way around the cobwebs and tried to open the door. I almost giggled when I found it locked. I sidestepped the door and entered through a hole in the wall. Pushing dusty boards out of my way, I looked around the living room. Mamaw had long since taken things off the walls and removed the braided rugs and furniture, but her presence lived in the room. Despite the absence of his tobacco, I could still smell the scent of Papaw's pipe in the air. I wasn't sure if the walls had soaked it in or if my memories affected my nostrils, but I inhaled anyway.

I walked to the kitchen at the back of the house. To my surprise, the dented metal cup that we drank from still hung on a wire on the wall above the sink. I swiped away a cobweb and unhooked it. I cupped it in my hands and closed my eyes.

"Tara Gail, you be sure and put that back on the wall when you finish." I turned and saw Mamaw wearing an apron, wiping her hands.

"Yes, ma'am" I whispered to the empty room. But I didn't put the cup back. I tucked it into my bag.

I walked around to the spot where her little table used to be, where she read her Bible in the morning with her coffee.

"Don't ever make a decision without consulting this first," she said, tapping the Bible with her reading glasses. "Your heart will lie to you, people will lie to you, but God's Word never lies."

I sighed and walked back to the living room. I looked where Papaw's chair used to be. I remembered his last words to me and realized I had probably disappointed him and Mamaw.

"You disappointed me, too, you know. Both of you!" I yelled out to the empty space. The echo haunted me. "Why didn't you help me? You and your family loyalty! What about me? I am your family, too!" I dropped to my knees and allowed the anguish of sorrow, guilt, and the sadness of what could have been flow out with my tears.

"Tara Gail, is that you?"

I jumped to my feet in surprise.

"Mama!" I resisted the urge to embrace her.

She stood at the front door. "What are you doing here?"

"I...I came back to see a friend."

She eyed me suspiciously. "Where have you been?"

"It doesn't matter, Mama." I dusted off my jeans.

"Why were you crying in the middle of the floor? Don't tell me you're sad they're going to tear down this place. It's not like you've been around anyway."

"You told me to get out, Mama. Remember?"

"You had to get out. I couldn't let you disrespect your mama. Not in my house."

Some things never changed. She made no move to hug her daughter whom she hadn't seen in eight years.

"I just wanted to take one more look. I do have memories here."

"Yeah, I know. She never forgave me, you know."

"Who? Mamaw? Forgave you for what?" I wanted to say for which offense, but I didn't.

"Taking you back. She hated me for it."

"I doubt that Mama. She packed my things as soon as you said we were going."

"You didn't hear the fight."

"What fight?"

"Oh, it doesn't really matter now. Anyway, she's gone. Daddy's gone. Brody's gone. Even the boys are gone. Soon this house will be gone, too." She looked around the room. I saw the pronounced lines on her cheeks. The last eight years were definitely unkind to her. Or maybe the truth was, she hadn't been kind to herself.

"What friend?"

"What?"

"You said you came to see a friend. Who?"

"You don't know her, Mama." Just like you don't know me, I thought.

"Oh. Okay. Well, I guess that's that, isn't it?"

"Are you still seeing Ted?"

"What? No. He's been long gone. You know me. If it's one thing I'm good at, it's driving people away."

I saw something in her eyes I had never seen before. Vulnerability. I recognized that look. I saw it every day when I looked in the mirror.

"I gotta go, Mama." I didn't say it was good to see her.

"Aren't you even going to let me know where you are?"

I stopped. Her words angered me. I turned around and looked at the woman I feared for so many years. The woman I both hated and loved and longed to please every day of my life. She looked small and frail standing in the middle of the dim, dusty room.

"Why? So you can control someone again? It won't work, Mama. You can't control me anymore. You. This place. You're all just memories to me now."

"You think because you're out of my house and grown that you don't need me? I'm your mama. You'll always need me. You never were anything special, Tara. That's your problem, though. You think you should be."

"You're wrong. I don't need you. I don't need you to think I'm special, either. But do you know what I just figured out? You need me. You've always needed me. You needed me to be your scapegoat for your guilt. You needed to degrade me so you could feel better about hating yourself."

"Why would I hate myself?"

"For so many reasons, Mama. But I'll give you just one. Reverend Martin."

She narrowed her eyes. "You think you're so much better than me? What is your life like? Go ahead, Tara. Tell me what you've been doing all these years." Her words cut as deep as she meant them to. How did she know? Did she recognize herself in my eyes, too?

"I'm a chef, Mama. I cook at a restaurant."

"Right. You're my daughter, Tara. I can tell when you're leaving out something. You're not telling the whole story."

I hated the truth in her words. But mostly I hated the resemblance in us I could no longer ignore.

"Think what you want, Mama. Like you said, you're good at driving people away."

I took one last look around the room, and then I left her standing in the middle of the memories.

I didn't go back to Onnie's right away. I walked down to the church where Mama took me before she ran off. I don't know what drew me there. Maybe I needed to confront everything from my childhood. It surprised me to find that they still didn't lock the church door. The sanctuary looked so small compared to my memories where it seemed so much bigger. I looked at the pew where Cindy and I giggled together and wrote notes on gum wrappers. Seeing her had been the highlight of the church services. I looked at another pew where she sat with another girl. I recalled the day I watched them giggle and laugh at me. I looked up to the pulpit and saw his eyes boring into mine. I saw the looks he often exchanged with my mother. I walked over to the piano where dear Mrs. Martin sat. I saw her gentle smile and her sad eyes.

As I turned to leave, there was another room I knew I had to face. Already the sounds of the southern gospel music filled my mind. I walked into the foyer then turned left toward the classrooms. The smell of crayons and glue halted my steps. Nausea hit me as soon as I opened the classroom door. The room looked exactly the same. Only the storyboards and bulletin boards had changed. The banner over the chalkboard had been there all this time. It read, "Jesus loves the little children". And there, right under that chalkboard and banner is where it had happened. I could still smell the sickly smell of him. I could still feel his weight crushing my small frame while he ignored my whimpering cries. I still tasted the butterscotch. I looked back up at that banner.

"You never loved me." I whispered. I turned and saw the poster on the wall. "Forgive one another even as Christ forgave you." I read aloud.

"Forgave me? Forgave me!" I yelled and cried. "How about I need to forgive you? Huh? What about that, Lord? How about I don't forgive you!"

I ran from the classroom, down the hall, and out the door as fast as I could. I ran all the way to Onnie's house, but I knew no matter how fast or how far I ran I'd never outrun the hate in my heart. For the first time in my life, I admitted it. I didn't hate my mama. I didn't hate the preacher. I didn't even hate the Candy Man.

I hated God.

# 25

Onnie's therapy worked. Her speech improved and her steps became a bit steadier. I had been there a week but didn't want to leave her yet.

On an unusually cool day, we went for a short walk on her street. Onnie held my arm and used the cane the doctor had given her, but she made it clear she didn't like it.

"Tara," she said.

I raised my eyes from watching her steps to meet her deep brown eyes. She spoke with pauses between her words.

"Tara...you...came...home...need...to..." she said, breathing in and out.

"Onnie, take your time. Do you want to stop?"

She nodded and pointed to her front porch steps. We made it there in minutes and sat down.

"Tara...you home...to ...fight ...demons."

"What?"

"Fight. Demons."

"I don't understand, Onnie."

She slapped the cane down in frustration and motioned for me to take her back into the house.

I walked her to the kitchen table, and she exhaled as she lowered herself onto the chair. She waved me to the other chair, so I sat, too. Pointing to her worn, large print Bible, she spoke again.

"Can't fight." She paused. "Can't without ..." She tapped the Bible.

"Onnie, please don't tire yourself."

She rubbed her eyes. "I'm...sorry, Tara."

"For what? What are you sorry for?"

"I should...I should have taken you...." She shook her head and pounded the table. "Home."

"It's okay, Onnie. I don't blame you. I know why you didn't."

"Didn't. I could have." She wiped tears from her eyes.

"I'm fine now, Onnie. Really. I'm okay."

She shook her head again. "No. Your eyes. Sad. I'm so... sorry."

"Oh, Onnie." I jumped up and hugged her tightly. She patted me and we cried together.

I sat back down, and she smiled at me. "You go to church."

"No, Onnie. It's not for me. You know that."

"You go to church." She said again. "For me."

I sighed. "Onnie..."

She wrote something down on a notepad and pointed to it. *Seventy times seven.*

"No, Onnie. You don't understand everything. God has no right to ask me to forgive all of them. He knew what they'd do to me. He knew what my mama would do, but He didn't protect me."

She stared hard at me, then wrote something else down. *Cotton is strongest when it's wet.*

"Onnie, what does that have to do with this?"

"God...He allows...for good."

I stood up in anger. "He allows for good? That's all you've got? Look at you, Onnie. You are the kindest, best woman I've ever known; yet here you are. Broken down to nothing. How can that be good?"

She shook her head and closed her eyes. "This...brought you home. Brought Clarissa."

Guilt slammed into my anger and the two exploded. "So, what, you think God gave you a stroke so you wouldn't be alone?

He gave me a mama who never cared, who physically and verbally abused me? Who let men abuse me for years? Even church men? Why did he do that? What 'good' came from any of that? To make me stronger?" I formed quote signs with my fingers.

"Oh, baby." She shook her head and cried, and I realized what I had just revealed to her.

"And what about Darren? Why did he allow that? Darren never hurt anybody. He just wanted to meet his grandfather. A grandfather who beat his wife and daughter. He wanted to connect because he had the kindest heart of any man I ever knew. Why did he have to die so horribly, Onnie? Stabbed to death in that nasty, dark place."

She started to speak, but I stopped her. "No. I can't listen to anymore. I'm sorry, Onnie. I need to get out of here." I pushed my chair in and left her sitting alone.

---

I don't know how or why I ended up back in that room. I looked at the Jesus banner over the chalkboard. I looked at the forgiveness poster. I looked at the spot on the floor where he stole my innocence while my mama laughed with the preacher down the hall.

"Hello, Tara."

I turned at the voice that startled me.

"Mrs. Martin?"

"Yes, it's me."

Puzzled, I frowned. "Why are you...did you follow me?"

She chuckled. "No, dear. I have a Sunday school class across the hall. I came to switch out my bulletin board."

"You still go here?"

"Not for a while, but I came back."

"Why? I never wanted to come back here. Especially here." I looked at the spot.

"It was that night, wasn't it, Tara? The night you were sick and came home with me?"

I said nothing. She continued.

"I knew something had happened. I just didn't know how to get to the bottom of it. I failed you, I'm afraid. It's just that...well, there was a lot going on that night."

I looked back up. "I'm sorry. I'm sorry about what she did to you."

"He did it, too, Tara. He had a choice."

"I know, but Mama..."

"Yes, your mama did her part, but they both were guilty."

"I'm sorry."

"You have no reason to be sorry."

"Why are you here? Doesn't it bother you?"

"No. This church rallied around me after they left together. Only a couple of members said things and acted nasty. That time you saw me? Well, that version of me didn't last long. These people didn't allow it. They gathered around and took turns supporting me and snapping me out of my dark place. I'm so thankful for this church, Tara. They didn't blame or shame me like I assumed they would. I realized I had treated them unfairly, assuming the worst of all of them because of a few."

"Well, I'm glad you're okay."

"Have you seen her, your mama?"

I nodded. "Briefly. At my grandparents' old place. Have you seen her?"

"No. I guess it's best for her sake."

"For her sake?"

"It has to be harder on her than on me, Tara. She carries the shame."

"She's never been ashamed of anything."

"Don't be so sure. Shame can disguise itself in many ways."

I shrugged. "It doesn't matter. She made her bed."

"True. But don't make your place beside her."

"What do you mean?"

"Her shame isn't yours. Let it go. Let all of it go." She waved her hand at the room.

"I don't know how to do that."

"You don't have to. He does." She pointed at the Jesus sign, then gave me a quick embrace.

I stood at the trailer and knocked. I heard scuffling inside and braced myself to see her again.

Her eyes widened when she opened the door. "Well, I didn't expect to see you again."

"I just came by to tell you goodbye."

"I thought you already did."

"Mama, can I come in?"

"Okay." She stepped aside and I walked into the haze of cigarette smoke and the odor from old ashes from ashtrays. "I don't have any money."

"I don't want money."

"Yeah, I guess I can see that." She looked me up and down and smirked. "So, what do you want?"

"I just wanted to see you before I go, that's all."

I saw something flicker in her gaze, but it disappeared quickly.

"Feeling guilty about treating me the way you did? Well, don't bother. When you left, life sure got easier, I can tell you."

"Is there anything you need, Mama?"

"Need?" She laughed. "From you? Don't you think you're something, coming here with those fancy clothes and making out like you gotta help me. Well, you ought to help me. All those years I took care of you and then you left the way you did. And for what? All because I mentioned Stanley's name..."

"He molested me, Mama. Over and over while you spent the night with Glenn."

"What?"

"Stanley. He molested me. For three years."

She stared at me, then picked up a cigarette and lit it. She puffed and stared at me through the smoke.

"If that's true, then why tell me now? What can I do about it?"

"If it's true? How can you say that?"

"You always made up stuff, Tara. What am I supposed to think?"

"You're supposed to believe your daughter for once. For once in your life, believe me."

"Alright, I believe you. I believe that you enticed him, always prancing your little butt in front of the men, teasing them with your tight jeans."

I stood up and looked down at her. "I suppose you hitting me, beating me, punching me, kicking me, and shoving me into cold water for as long as I can remember was my fault, too? Or how about the time you banged my head into a brick wall until I passed out? Throwing things at me, and oh, my favorite, shoving food down my throat because you thought I didn't eat enough. Not to mention all the nasty things you said to me, even calling me names as far back as I can remember. Was all of that my fault, too?"

"You're darned right it was your fault! Do you think you were an easy kid? Worked my fingers to the bone and then came home to a sniffling brat. But you don't even remember the nice things I did. Birthday parties, shopping trips, board games. I did all kinds of nice things with you."

"Forget it, Mama. Forget I said anything." I walked to the door then turned back around. I dug into the purse on my arm and pulled out a fifty dollar bill. I tossed it on the coffee table. Then, I walked around to where she sat and bent down to kiss her cheek. She flinched, but I saw a hint of helpless confusion in her eyes. I walked back to Onnie's house, realizing Mrs. Martin had been right. Shame is often disguised. I also realized she had been right about something else. Until now I had been making my place beside Mama in her bed of shame.

# *Epilogue*

T he Sunday before I went home, I walked into church beside Onnie. Black, smiling faces welcomed their friend back. They stared at me as I held her arm. Perhaps I was the first white person to enter their church, but I met smiling eyes as I helped Onnie to her pew.

I didn't know exactly what I was doing there, but I walked a bit lighter that day. I hadn't yet reconciled with God or my mother, or any of the men who had wronged me, but I now had hope that I might because I was willing to try. I wanted to know who the real Jesus was. The one Chris and Onnie and Mrs. Martin knew.

Onnie and I sat down on the third pew. She didn't stand to sing, but it didn't stop her from clapping along as her brothers and sisters sang with raised arms and swaying bodies. Their energy proved contagious. My foot tapped along to their claps.

The preacher sounded like a mix of Martin Luther King, Jr., and Billy Graham. I found myself listening to a sermon for the first time in my life.

"Jesus died for your soul. He died for my soul. But you know who else He died for? That ugly soul. That soul you can't forgive. But of course, you can't forgive him. Only the Son of God can give that power to you if you're willing to let Him. So Let Him, dear brother. Let Him, dear sister."

Onnie reached over and squeezed my hand. I squeezed back.

"You ask me like the disciple asked our Lord. How many times do I have to forgive that ugly soul when they hurt me over and over and over again? And I'll say to you, dear brother. I'll say to you, dear sister, I'll say this. Seventy times seven. In other words, there is no limit. And you don't have to have no limit when you let the power of His grace flow from you. It's not for them. You're not condoning what they did to you. You're releasing it to Christ. So, how many times?" He held his hand to his ear. The congregation shouted, "Seventy times seven!" They raised their hands and shouted again.

"How many?" The preacher asked again.

"Seventy times seven," I whispered with their shouts.

I didn't know if I could forgive tomorrow. I didn't know if it'd be the day after that. But I realized that Onnie had been right all along. The rain in my life had strengthened me. I just had to soak it in rather than repel it. Running had done me no good at all. I had to come back before I could move forward. And I was ready to move forward. Tomorrow I'd have to face going back to Mandeville, to the restaurant and to my new, old life. I'd have to face going back to Chris. I didn't like the nerves in my stomach at the thought of seeing him again now that he knew the truth about my past, but the preacher's words gave me hope for tomorrow no matter what was waiting for me there. After all, tomorrow was another day.

# A Note from the Author

D ear Reader,

I hope Tara's story encouraged you to seek hope in forgiveness for any wrongs that have been committed against you. It is in forgiveness that we finally let go of the pain and begin to heal. Sometimes life isn't always a neatly, wrapped package. We may find that even when we forgive, reconciliation with that person doesn't necessarily follow. However, we can always be reconciled to Christ. Sometimes forgiving is a continual process rather than a single act. Tara learned that she might have to forgive many times, or that she might have to try many times to forgive once.

Tara's life was filled with injustices and abuse. Not only from those who abused her, but also from those who stayed silent or didn't act on her behalf. Many times, victims of abuse are more likely to be abused again and again. Maybe that is your story today, or in the past, or both. Know that hope is available. You do not have to suffer in silence anymore. You do not have to continue to be a victim.

There are other themes to this story, and maybe they touched you as well. Racism, dysfunctional families, and the good and badly flawed dynamics of the church, all have a place in our own world. Perhaps Tara's story has helped you if you have dealt with any of these difficult issues.

If you'd like to discuss this story or any other story I've written, please contact me: fayla@faylaott.com. I love hearing feedback from my readers! If you liked this story, please consider leaving a review on Amazon and Goodreads. Reviews help authors get more readers.

Thanks in advance for your help.

And thank you for reading!

*Fayla Ott*

# About the Author

F ayla Ott began writing at an early age. Before she could even read, she would look at picture books and make up her own stories to match the pictures. As a teen, she filled notebooks with poems, short stories, and essays. She graduated with a Bachelor of Arts degree in English from the University of Maryland, and then with a Master of Arts degree in English from National University.

Fayla is married and has two boys. She also has two stepsons, a daughter-in-law, and three grandchildren. She lives in the Great Smoky Mountains of East Tennessee. When she is not writing, she teaches college English courses online and home schools her youngest son. Her hobbies include reading, cooking, hiking, singing in her church choir, playing piano and guitar, and spending time with her family. She enjoys the adventures of traveling, too, and does so any chance she gets.

Fayla's desire for her writing is that it draws others closer to Jesus Christ, and that she can worship Him through her stories.

If you'd like to contact Fayla, email her at faylaott@gma il.com, or follow her on Facebook, Instagram, Amazon, and

Goodreads. You can also visit her website at www.faylaott.co
m.

# Connect with Fayla Online